KILLER INSIGHT

VIRGINIA VAUGHAN

D0004213

LOVE INSPIRED SUSPENSE

INSPIRATIONAL ROMANCE

LOVE INSPIRED® SUSPENSE
INSPIRATIONAL ROMANCE

ISBN-13: 978-1-335-40264-6

Killer Insight

Copyright © 2020 by Virginia Vaughan

Recycling programs
for this product may
not exist in your area.

This edition published by arrangement with Harlequin Books S.A.

For questions and comments about the quality of this book,
please contact us at CustomerService@Harlequin.com.

Love Inspired
22 Adelaide St. West, 40th Floor
Toronto, Ontario M5H 4E3, Canada
www.Harlequin.com

Printed in U.S.A.

"There's nothing you could tell me that would change the way I feel about you..."

Lucy wanted to believe that. Bryce was a good and loyal man. How she wanted to lean into him! She fought her own instincts. She had to.

Bruce took the room key from her. "Let me check the room before you go inside."

He pulled his gun from his holster and pushed open the door, flicking on the light. He opened the bathroom door and, when he did, a blast of gunfire sent Lucy flying backwards. She hit the wall and had the breath knocked from her.

Bryce was holding his shoulder and blood was pooling between his fingers.

Lucy grabbed up Bryce's gun from the floor and kicked open the bathroom door, but all she saw was a rifle hanging from a wire attached to the ceiling. There was no shooter, only an elaborate booby trap.

"I'm calling for an ambulance."

"I'm not leaving you," he barked. "Someone set a booby trap in your room. That was meant for you, Lucy."

Whoever had set this trap had intended to kill her.

Bryce had taken the bullet that was meant for her.

Virginia Vaughan is a born-and-raised Mississippi girl. She is blessed to come from a large Southern family, and her fondest memories include listening to stories recounted around the dinner table. She was a lover of books from a young age, devouring tales of romance, danger and love. She soon started writing them herself. You can connect with Virginia through her website, virginiavaughanonline.com, or through the publisher.

Books by Virginia Vaughan

Love Inspired Suspense

Covert Operatives

Cold Case Cover-Up
Deadly Christmas Duty
Risky Return
Killer Insight

Rangers Under Fire

Yuletide Abduction
Reunion Mission
Ranch Refuge
Mistletoe Reunion Threat
Mission Undercover
Mission: Memory Recall

No Safe Haven

He will turn again, he will have compassion upon us;
he will subdue our iniquities; and thou wilt
cast all their sins into the depths of the sea.
–*Micah* 7:19

This book is dedicated to my friends and family,
without whom this writing gig wouldn't be possible.

ONE

FBI agent Lucy Sanderson stopped running, rested her hands on her knees and tried to catch her breath. She'd pushed herself on this run, harder than she had in weeks, and her body was pushing back. She glanced around. She'd run farther than she'd planned, and not being familiar with this town, she was uncertain where she was.

She shouldn't have come so far, or she should have turned back when the streetlights stopped being consistently spaced, but she'd been anxious to get her run in. She needed to get back in shape after letting her regimen lapse for months after her fiancé Danny's death last year, and her legs ached after the flight down from Washington, DC, then the hour-long drive to the small Texas town of Whitten.

Lucy glanced at her watch. It was after 7:00 p.m., and she really should get back to the bed-and-breakfast where she was staying. Her meeting with Bryce Tippitt, an old marine friend of Danny's who'd reached out to her for help, was in less than an hour. His brother was accused of killing four women in this sleepy Texas town, but Bryce insisted his brother was innocent and being railroaded by the local police department. She'd agreed to come, anxious to put her FBI-trained profiling skills back to work after the paralyzing self-doubt that had set in after Danny's death and she'd learned the truth about her fiancé and the lies he'd been telling her.

She shoved her earbuds back in and music filled her ears, drowning out the sounds of nature as she started her run back toward town. It was time to stop sitting on the sidelines and pick up her stalled career where Danny's death had left it. Her supervisor had encouraged her to come to Whitten, anxious to get her back into profiling, insisting she was good at what she did. Not good enough, however, to see what had been right in front of her face.

Headlights rolled over her, and she glanced over a shoulder to see a car approaching. Lucy moved to the side of the road for it to pass, even though the roadway was clear and there was no oncoming traffic. Instead of speeding around her, the car slowed, then pulled to the side. She stopped and turned toward it, straining to see past the blinding headlights.

Suddenly a man leaped from the car. He was on top of her before she realized what was happening. He pinned her to the ground, and all of Lucy's instincts kicked in. She fought back, screaming and flailing and calling on every defensive move she'd learned at the academy. She managed to dig her nails into his skin, but, in the end, she was no match for his weight and strength. He pinned her with one arm and pulled a syringe from his pocket.

If he managed to inject her with it, she was done

for. She wiggled her arm free and knocked the syringe from his grip. Instead of retrieving it, he punched her several times. Her eyes watered from the pain as the world spun in and out of focus.

She was still dazed as he bound her hands with a zip tie then ripped her phone from the holder on her arm and jerked out her earbuds, throwing the items into the trees. He lifted her, tossing her across his shoulder like a sack of flour. He was quick and efficient, and her limbs felt like rocks as all the fight seemed to drain from her. She couldn't even cry out for help. Not that there was anyone around to help her. She was in an isolated area. *Rookie mistake.*

He shoved her into the trunk of his car and slammed the lid, plunging her completely into darkness. Her mind was still working, racing with the thought that she needed to run, to get away, but her body refused to work, still in shock from such a brutal attack.

She was going to die tonight at the hands of the very killer she'd been sent here to stop. The irony of it rushed through her as the brake lights illuminated the trunk in their bright red color and the car took off.

But she wasn't ready to give up.

Lucy fought to stay awake when blissful uncon-sciousness pulled at her. She couldn't succumb to it. If she did, she was dead. She fumbled, her hands search-ing for some way to free herself from the vehicle. Fi-nally she found the trunk lever. She pushed it and the lid unlatched, bobbing ever so slightly up and down as the car moved along the asphalt.

She could jump free, but not until the car slowed enough. If he caught her and she was injured escaping, she would be in real trouble. But if she waited too long, he might discover the trunk lid unlatched, and her one opportunity for escape would be gone.

The car slowed then turned. Lucy raised up on her elbows to peek out. They were turning onto a dirt road. That wasn't a good sign. She needed to go now while there might still be traffic in the area so she could flag down someone to help her. The deeper into the woods they drove, the less likely she was to find her way out.

She had to go now.

Lucy shoved open the trunk and jumped out, landing hard on her right ankle. Intense pain shot through her leg, but she didn't have time to stop and examine her foot. She could still put weight on it, although she would be considerably slower than she would have liked.

A sharp pain through her temple nearly knocked her to the ground. She stumbled into a tree. Her vision was still blurry, and the world was spinning. He'd hit her hard, and she thought she was likely feeling the effects of a concussion. She had to push through. She had no idea where she was or which direction she was heading. All she knew was she had to put some distance between herself and that car.

Lucy heard the squeal of brakes and turned back to look. The car had stopped and the man jumped from the front seat, rifle in hand. She turned and ran as hard as she could, ignoring the pain in her foot or the way the world seemed to change directions. Branches bit into her face and arms, but she didn't stop. She couldn't stop.

Her abductor had the advantage. He might know these woods, and she was running blind and injured. She heard him behind her, chasing her. She recalled the road they'd turned off and knew she had to reach it. She could get lost in these woods and never be heard from again. Her only choice, if she wanted to stay alive, was reaching the road and flagging down a car for help.

Lucy climbed over the embankment and onto the road as headlights appeared in the distance. Relief washed over her. She hurried onto the pavement and waved her arms to try to catch the attention of the driver.

The approaching truck slammed on its brakes and skidded to a halt right in front of her. The driver's-side door opened and a man jumped out.

"What do you think you're doing?"

She nearly fell at his feet with relief, but he grabbed her arms and held her up. "Help me. Please help me!" she cried. "He's after me."

His blue eyes studied her. She was certain her face was swollen and bloody from the beating she'd taken, and he couldn't help noticing her hands were bound. He glanced around, then took her elbow and ushered her into the cab of his truck.

A girl of about thirteen, her young eyes wide with fear and shock, helped pull her onto the seat. "Are you okay? What happened?"

Lucy scrambled across the seat. "A man. He's chasing me."

She noticed the look that passed between the young girl and the man who slid into the driver's seat and slammed the door.

"You're safe now," the girl stated. "My name's Meghan, and that's my dad, Bryce. He'll protect you. He used to be a marine."

"This man," Bryce said. "What did he look like?"

She turned to answer him, but noticed movement outside the window. A man stood just clear of the tree line. He scanned the area, then raised his rifle.

"That's him!" she shouted as he fired. Instinct kicked in, she grabbed the girl and flung them both to the floorboards as a bullet sliced through the windshield, buzzed past her and shattered the back glass.

She couldn't believe he was still coming after her, even with two witnesses. Bryce's demeanor was calm even as he sprang into action. He jammed the truck into reverse and hit the accelerator, his expression set even as a second bullet burst through the glass. Lucy lowered her head and shielded the girl as best she could as Bryce quickly turned the truck around and floored it. Another shot rang out, but this one was fainter and she knew he'd managed to put some distance between them and the shooter.

"Are you both okay?" he asked, never letting up on the accelerator.

She glanced at Meghan, who nodded, then Lucy answered him. "We're okay." Only then did she notice blood dripping on the seat from a wound to his head. "You're hit." She crawled back onto the seat and examined the wound on his ear.

He touched his hand to his head and saw blood, then waved it off like it was nothing. "It's just a graze. I'll be fine."

"You need a hospital."

"I'm heading there now, using a different road into town." He reached into his pocket and pulled out a knife. Lucy jerked back, fear hurtling through her. She didn't know this man or what he would do to her. "It's okay," he reassured her. "I was just going to cut your binds."

She glanced at her hands, still bound by the zip tie, and realized how silly she was being. This man and his daughter had rescued her. If she hadn't run into him, her abductor might have caught up to her. She shuddered to think what would have happened to her then. She stared up into the soft blue of Bryce's eyes, noting also his square jaw and blond beard. He had a kind face, and something about Meghan's reassurance earlier that he'd been a marine comforted her. He'd certainly proven himself with the calm demeanor he'd maintained while being shot at. She held out her hands, and he quickly sliced through the zip tie.

"I don't remember seeing you before. What's your name?" he asked her.

"Lucy. Lucy Sanderson."

He turned to her, and it was his turn to be shocked. "Danny's fiancée? I was on my way to see you after I dropped Meghan off at a friend's house."

Realization dawned on her. This was the man who'd brought her to town. "You're Bryce Tippitt."

"I am. This is my daughter, Meghan."

"It's nice to meet you," the girl said.

"You too." Suddenly, she did feel safer. She'd never met Bryce, but Danny had spoken fondly of his leadership skills and loyalty, and she'd talked to him on the phone before coming to town. She might have placed his name or voice sooner if her head was clearer. That small connection gave her some level of comfort. The warmth of the heater flowed over her, helping to calm her too. She was safe now.

She took a deep breath, finally allowing the pain and terror of the last hour to grab hold. Her ankle ached, her head pounded and every muscle in her body felt like stone. But she was free. She'd escaped a killer. And she owed her life to this man and his daughter.

She settled back against the seat, closed her eyes and listened to the hum of road as the darkness she'd been fighting finally took her.

"Daddy, she's out!" Meghan yelled.

Bryce turned and saw Lucy's head bob as she lost consciousness. He pulled the truck to the shoulder, then turned to check Lucy's pulse. It was weak. "Lucy, wake up," Bryce said, shaking her petite shoulders. Her dark hair slipped over her face. All he'd seen of her face earlier that wasn't covered in dirt and blood was a pair of frightened green eyes staring back at him. He wished she would open them now. He was just noticing the dark bruise forming on her face, along with multiple scratches and a busted lip. Someone had beaten her. He tried to reassure his daughter. "She's been running on adrenaline. It's wearing off. She'll be fine once we get her to the hospital." He put the truck back into gear and took off again.

They were taking a longer route to town around the river, but he wasn't about to turn and go back the other way, not when a maniac with a gun was out there. He was probably long gone by now, having missed his chance to follow them, but Bryce wasn't taking any chances.

He dialed 911 on his cell phone, told the operator who answered what had happened and where they were headed, and she promised to have someone from the police department meet them at the hospital.

"Dad, the guy that attacked Lucy. Was it…?" Meghan's voice was low and soft and she couldn't finish the question, but he knew she was asking about the killer on the loose. It was a sad day when even thirteen-year-olds had to be worried about their own safety.

"We don't know that," he said, trying to reassure her, but was implying someone else was out there preying on women any better than knowing one killer was on the loose? His stomach rolled at the thought of what she'd escaped from. "Probably," he conceded.

Bryce's heart hammered against his chest. They'd encountered the man the press had dubbed the Back Roads Killer, the man who'd caused the deaths his brother was accused of. His gut churned thinking how close his daughter had been to that madman. His next thought was anger as he realized he couldn't even identify the man who'd shot at them. Another opportunity to bring the real killer to justice, and he'd missed it.

Or maybe they hadn't. He glanced at the woman on the seat beside him. What tale would she have when she awoke? Would she be able to describe her attacker? To his knowledge, she was the first to escape, the first who might be able to put a name and a face to the man who had terrorized this town for over a year.

His eyes fell on his brother's contact number on his phone, and dread pumped through him. He pushed the speed dial for Clint's number, each ring sending waves of worry through him. Finally the call rolled over to voice mail, and Bryce left a message telling his brother to call him ASAP.

He shouldn't be making so many calls while driving, but reaching his brother was important. The local police had zeroed in on Clint as their prime suspect in the murders because his girlfriend, Jessica, had been the first victim, but his brother was no killer. Would someone from the FBI with no preconceived ideas about Clint have a fresh perspective and see this case for what it was? That had been his hope when he'd reached out to her for help. Would she be able to finally clear his brother's name? She already had an advantage no one else had had before. She'd seen and escaped the attacker. He'd been burned before by government types who'd promised to help him then did nothing, yet he still dared to hope this time would be different. It was all he could do.

Police lights in his mirror caught his attention. A police cruiser pulled up beside him and motioned for him to roll down the window. He recognized the officer in the passenger's seat as Jacob Newell.

He rolled down his window and Jacob spoke to him over the roar of the road. "Follow us to the hospital. We'll escort you." The police cruiser turned on its sirens and roared away. Bryce hit the accelerator and followed, all the while sending up prayers that when this beautiful brunette beside him awoke, she would be able to point the finger at her attacker, catch a killer who had preyed on his town for too long and clear his brother's name once and for all. It was a lot to ask, but she'd already proven she was strong. Strong enough to escape a killer.

They arrived at the emergency room, and Lucy was whisked away on a gurney while Bryce was ushered into a curtained area to have his ear examined. He hadn't even realized he'd been shot until Lucy pointed it out. His own adrenaline had gone on high alert when he'd seen the gunman. It hadn't been his first firefight by any means—he'd seen plenty during his time as a marine and while working covert security for the CIA as part of the Special Operations Abroad team, or SOA—but his daughter had been with him and his main concern had been getting her to safety…her and the woman who'd pushed Meghan to the floorboards before he could even react. He hadn't missed that unselfish act. She'd escaped a killer but had thought of another person when the shooting started.

Meghan stayed close by his side, her worry evident despite his assurances that he wasn't hurt badly. He put his arm around her and pulled her to him. She was shaking, and rightly so. No one so young should ever have to witness what she had, or experience being shot at.

"We're okay now," he assured her.

"What about Lucy?" she asked.

The curtain flung open and Cassidy Summers, Bryce's longtime friend and a nurse at the hospital, stood there looking surprised and worried. "What happened?" she asked as she walked in and removed the gauze the first attendant had placed over his ear to stop the bleeding.

"We found a woman on the road," Meghan told her. "She'd been attacked and kidnapped, but she escaped and flagged us down. Then he started shooting at us!"

Cassidy shot Bryce a look. "It's true then? I've heard people saying someone escaped the Back Roads Killer.

The whole hospital has been in an uproar about it since the call came in."

Bryce nodded. "It is true. Her name is Lucy Sanderson. She's an FBI profiler. I asked her to come to town to help me prove Clint's innocence. Instead, she was nearly killed by that maniac."

Cassidy examined his ear. "It's only a graze. You don't even need stitches. I'll bandage you up, and you can head home."

"Daddy, can't we stay and check on Lucy? I want to make certain she's okay."

He had the same concern. "We will, Meghan. I want to know too. Besides, I'm the one who invited her here. I feel responsible."

A commotion in the lobby caused Cassidy to push back the curtain. Several reporters with TV cameras and sound equipment were setting up in the waiting area. Cassidy groaned. "The newspeople are here already. That was quick."

He stood and pulled on his jacket. "News spreads fast in this town. Wait until they learn she's with the FBI." He turned to Cassidy. "Thanks for patching me up. Do you know where they took Lucy?"

"Down the hall to the last room on the left." She grabbed his arm, pulling him back from barreling ahead. "Bryce, Meghan really shouldn't be here around this craziness. Shouldn't you take her home?"

Cassidy was always his voice of reason, but Bryce knew his daughter was too kindhearted to be able to leave without making sure Lucy was okay first. "I will after we know Lucy is okay."

The disapproving look on her face told him she

didn't think he was making the smart choice to drag his thirteen-year-old daughter along with him, but she didn't argue the point.

He grabbed Meghan's hand and followed Cassidy down the hallway as Jim Ross, a detective with the local task force set up to find the Back Roads Killer, stepped in front of the reporters and issued a statement about the night's events.

Cassidy stopped in front of the door. "Wait here. I'll go inside and see if the doctor is still with her."

Bryce agreed and pulled out his cell phone, trying his brother again while they waited. Once again, the call went straight to voice mail. Where was Clint, and why wasn't he answering his phone?

Lucy had been frightened when she woke up in the hospital with no memory of how she'd gotten there. But then the pieces started coming back to her. The blitz attack. Being beaten and dumped into the trunk of a car. Escaping and being shot at. And the handsome marine and his daughter who'd rescued her.

The nurse spoke in a hushed tone to another nurse, then walked to her bed. "You've got some people wanting to see you. Are you up for it?"

Lucy nodded. She owed her life to Bryce Tippitt and his daughter, and she was anxious to hear if they were both all right.

Meghan hurried into the room, followed by Bryce and another man she didn't recognize. Meghan rushed to the bed and threw her arms around Lucy. "I'm so glad you're okay."

Lucy was surprised by the affectionate act, but assured her she was fine.

"I'm glad you're feeling better," Bryce said, standing beside her bed, his head cocked in a concerned manner as his steely blue eyes watched her.

"I owe you my life, Bryce Tippitt. You and your daughter." She reached for his hand and clasped it, a comfortable warmth flowing through her.

"I'm glad we were there to help."

Meghan beamed with pride as the other man stepped forward.

"Ma'am, I'm Detective Jim Ross, head of the Back Roads Killer task force."

She shuddered at the name they'd given this offender. The Back Roads Killer. It seemed to fit. She'd met him and nearly become his latest victim.

"I'd like to ask you what you remember about the attack."

"We should give you some privacy," Bryce stated, pulling his hand from Lucy's, but her instincts kicked in and she pulled it back.

"Please don't leave me." It was an irrational request that came out of nowhere, but after what she'd endured tonight, she felt better having this handsome almost-stranger around at least until she got her bearings again. Her safety seemed to depend upon his presence. His daughter's words replayed in her mind. *You're safe now. He'll protect you. He used to be a marine.*

He hesitated, and she realized it was too much to ask. He had somewhere else to be, and she was imposing on his time. He had his daughter with him, and she suddenly realized he needed to see to her. She pulled her hand away and started to take back her request when he tightened his grip.

"I'll stay for as long as you need." He looked past Lucy to his daughter. "But you should wait outside." He motioned one of the nurses, who stepped forward.

"I'll take her. Come on, Meghan."

The girl protested. "Do I have to? Can't I please stay for a while longer?"

"No. This is police business."

"Can I come back to see you?" Meghan asked, and Lucy was glad for it.

"Absolutely. Anytime."

Once they'd left the room, Detective Ross turned to her. "I need you to tell me exactly what happened tonight."

Lucy sat up in the bed, ignoring the pounding in her head and the pain snaking up her ankle. She needed to recall every detail as clearly as she could, knowing that the smallest thing could lead them to the killer. "I arrived in town about five this afternoon and decided to take a run before meeting Bryce. I realized it was getting late, so I turned around near an old gas station to head back to town. That's when I noticed a car heading for me. It slowed down then stopped, and a man jumped out, grabbed me, then pinned me down and tried to inject something into my neck, but I managed to knock it from his hand so he hit me instead. I was barely conscious when he put me in the trunk of his car. I'm not sure how long I was in it, but I was eventually able to pop the trunk and run for help. That's when I flagged down Bryce and Meghan."

"Did you see the man's face?"

She saw Bryce tense and stand at attention in response to the question. She strained to remember something notable about the man, but it had all happened so quickly. She shook her head. "I think there was something covering it. He was wearing a hat low, but something about his face was obscured."

Bryce slouched again, and she felt his disappointment and remembered she was here because his brother was the main suspect in this case. He'd probably been hoping she could identify her attacker as someone else.

"Where did this occur?" Detective Ross asked.

"I—I don't know. I'm not familiar with this town. If I can see a map, I might be able to pick out the area."

Ross pulled up a map of town on his cell phone and handed it to her, pointing out where Mrs. Ferguson's B&B, the starting point for her run, was located for her to reference. She outlined the route she'd run, then estimated the place where the man had abducted her. "Right there. I turned around at that old service station. I'd only run a few minutes when the car approached me."

"I'll send a team out there to look for evidence. What about the vehicle? Can you describe it?"

"It was a sedan. Four doors. Silver, I think. Other than that, I didn't see much. It all happened so fast." She saw the look he gave her as he jotted the information in a notebook, and her face burned with embarrassment. She was an agent from the FBI. She should have had better observational skills. Yes, it had been dark and happened quickly, but she was a trained professional and should have noticed more details. Then she remembered something important. "I scratched him." Detective Ross glanced up at her, and Bryce stood at attention. "I scratched his arm. I felt my fingernails dig into it." She raised her hand to look at her fingernails as excitement bubbled through her. "I have his DNA under my fingernails."

Bryce's eyes brightened, matching her own excitement. "This is it," he said. "This is the proof we need to prove my brother's innocence and finally track down the real killer."

"I'll go find a lab tech to collect the samples," Ross said before walking out.

Bryce ran a hand over his face, beaming. She liked the way it looked. "You did it. When I asked you to come here and help me prove my brother's innocence, this wasn't what I had in mind, but you did it."

"It's not exactly what I had in mind either when I agreed to come." But that didn't matter anymore. While profiling had value and often helped identify suspects, physical evidence of her attacker could not be refuted.

Bryce pulled up a chair, careful not to touch her hands again until the lab technician could scrape beneath her nails. "I never told you how sorry I was about Danny's death. I had no idea when I contacted you."

His condolences caught her off guard, and she struggled to respond. She hadn't handled his death well, and even now, the mention of his name filled her with grief and guilt. "I should have reached out to his friends. I just— I just couldn't deal with telling people at the time."

"How did it happen?"

She was always uncomfortable with knowing how much to share about what had happened. "It was a car accident. He hit another car—a van—with a family inside. No one survived." She didn't tell him the rest. He deserved to think better of his friend, and what would he think of her profiling skills if he knew Danny had been under the influence of drugs when he hit that van or that she'd had no idea about his addiction to pain-killers? It didn't say much about her profiling skills that he'd fooled her for months.

Ross reentered the room with a lab technician who got busy scraping beneath her nails and collecting the skin samples.

"Send these to the FBI crime lab," Lucy told him. "I'll call my boss and have them fast-tracked. But even then, it'll be weeks before the results are back. In the meantime, I'd like to see the case files so I can work up a profile."

Ross nodded. "I'll have them copied and sent to you."

"When he contacted me, Bryce said the task force is focusing on his brother as their main suspect. How solid is the case against him?"

"It's mostly circumstantial. That's why we haven't been able to make an arrest yet. It's also the reason I was able to convince my chief to allow you to consult on this case. He's anxious for some solid leads. I told him you would be able to provide some. He wants to make an arrest before another woman dies."

"This evidence will prove my brother is innocent," Bryce insisted. "Your task force needs to turn its focus elsewhere."

"Right now, we're focusing on the leads we have. I'm heading out to the scene where you were attacked, Agent Sanderson." He set his card on the tray in front of her. "Call me if you think of anything else."

"I will."

He nodded to them both then headed out. Moments later the lab technician finished collecting her samples and left.

Lucy glanced at Bryce, now so excited for this new development that could prove his brother's innocence. She'd offered her services, but profiling wasn't an exact science. She might not be able to completely rule out Clint Tippitt as a suspect. DNA might do that…or it might prove his guilt. She wondered if Bryce was ready for that outcome. Did he believe in Clint, or was he foolishly blind to the truth? She'd been that way with Danny—blinded by love to who he really was—and people had died because of it. She hoped Bryce Tippitt wouldn't make the same mistake.

"I should go check on Meghan and make sure she gets home safely."

"Of course. Go. She needs you." She felt silly for her earlier exclamation asking him to stay. He had a responsibility to his daughter first and foremost. "I'll be fine."

"I would normally ask my friend Cassidy to take her. They spend a lot a time together. She's like a mother to Meghan, but she's working. I'll take her to her friend's house, then I'll come back afterward and check on you."

"You don't have to. I'm fine, Bryce. Really."

"I'll be back," he assured her. "In the meantime, I'm going to ask Cassidy to check up on you. She's the nurse who took Meghan out of here earlier. She'll take care of you."

She assured him again she was fine, and he left. She had to admit she was glad he was coming back. Silly or not, she felt better with him around. She didn't know if it was because he'd saved her life or because he was her only contact in town—or simply just her last, final connection to Danny. Whatever the reason, Bryce Tippitt and his daughter had made an impact on her. For the first time since Danny's death, she didn't feel quite so alone.

The door opened and a nurse entered, pushing a rolling cart loaded with bouquets of flowers. "These arrived for you," she said happily.

Lucy was confused. "Who are they from? Who even knows I'm here?" She didn't know anyone in town, and none of her friends or family back in Virginia could have known about the attack already.

"Honey, it's already all over the news that you were attacked and managed to escape. These are from well-wishers all over town."

She set a vase with flowers on the table beside the bed, and Lucy felt her eyes starting to water at the aroma of the fresh-cut flowers. "They're lovely, but I have allergies. Could you set them by the window where I can see them, but they're not close enough to aggravate my allergies?"

"Of course." She moved the flowers to the corner of the room, then pulled out the cards and handed them to Lucy so she could look through them. "If the police are done with their questioning, I'll see about getting you something for the pain so you can rest tonight. With no evidence of anything broken and only a mild concussion, the doctor says you'll probably be released in the morning."

Lucy was glad to hear it. She would also be glad to get out of this hospital bed and the gown and into regular clothes. Mostly, she would be glad to stop feeling like a victim and get back to finding the killer. Yes, they had his DNA, but it would take time for the lab results to come back, and until they did, the women of this town were still in danger.

She glanced at the cart of flowers. The scent was still tickling her nose, but they were far enough away to prevent a full-blown flare up. There were at least fifteen bouquets. Fifteen people who didn't know her but had heard about her predicament on the news and felt compelled to send her get-well flowers. Those small acts of kindness spoke more about this town than the killer on the loose did.

Lucy picked up the stack of note cards that had accompanied the flowers and looked through them. Most of the names she didn't know, but one stood out. Mrs. Ferguson, the owner of the B&B where she was staying, had sent her an arrangement. That was sweet—Lucy would be sure to thank her.

She flipped to the next card and the warm, comforting feeling she'd been floating on turned to chills. Beneath the buzzing bee symbol of the flower shop was a threat.

Next time you die.

Bryce dropped Meghan off at a friend's house for the night, then booked it back to the hospital. He knew he didn't have to stay with Lucy. The nurse had assured him she would rest most of the night. But he wanted to be there, since he was the one who'd brought her to town.

And it had nothing to do with the way her hand had felt so light and delicate in his. Nope. Nothing at all.

He tried to phone his brother again as he pulled into the hospital parking lot. There was still no answer from Clint, no response to his repeated text messages and no return call. He didn't like it. Another woman had been attacked, and his brother was MIA. It wouldn't look good if he couldn't explain where he'd been. The least Bryce could hope for was that his brother was somewhere that ten or twelve witnesses could place him for the whole night.

He hated that his mind went there. A woman was attacked in his town, and he was worried about his brother's alibi? It wasn't right, but it was the situation they found themselves in now. But the situation had changed for the better thanks to Lucy. She'd gotten DNA evidence from the man who'd attacked her, evidence that would prove beyond a shadow of a doubt that it wasn't Clint.

He headed to Lucy's room and found Jim Ross talking to her, along with two members of his forensics team.

"What's going on?" he asked as they were bagging up bouquets of flowers from a cart in the corner.

He noticed Lucy looked even paler than she had earlier, the bruise on her face darker and more pronounced. She held up an evidence bag with a card inside. "The nurse brought in all these flowers from well-wishers. This note was attached to one of them."

He didn't miss the way her hand shook as she held it out to him. He took the bag and looked at it, his blood going cold at the threat. "Do we know who sent this?"

"Not yet," Ross told him. "The nurse removed all the cards from the bouquets, so we don't even know which one it was attached to. I'm having my people bag all the flowers in case, and we'll run the card for fingerprints to see if we get a hit. Right now, that's all we can do. I've got most of my resources tied up at the abduction site gathering evidence. Once we're done with that, we'll interview the people at the flower shop."

"I'll do it," Lucy volunteered.

"I don't think that's a good idea," Ross countered. "You're the victim."

But she wasn't backing down. She squared her shoulders as she locked eyes with him. "I'm also an FBI agent trained in interview and interrogation. I want to do this." She pushed back the blankets and tried to stand. Bryce quickly helped her when her knees threatened to buckle. She clearly wasn't up for this tonight.

"I'll go with her," Bryce suggested. "But the shop will already be closed tonight." He glanced at Ross, who shrugged.

"Fine. Let me know if anything comes of it. Who would have a reason to threaten you?" Ross asked her.

"Besides the man who abducted and tried to murder me, you mean?"

"Yes, besides him."

Lucy sighed and settled back down on the bed, giving up the pretense of trying to stand. Good. She didn't need to push herself. "I don't know anyone in this town and, to my knowledge, the only people who knew I was coming were you and Bryce. Has this perpetrator reached out to the police or media before?"

Ross shook his head. "No. We've never received any form of communication from him."

"Then either learning the FBI was involved bolstered his ego, or else he meant this threat for me personally."

"The news has been broadcasting that you're FBI," Bryce told her. Her attack and escape from the killer were all anyone in town was talking about tonight. He'd even had to spend several minutes at Meghan's friend's house chitchatting about it with her mother before he'd been able to leave.

"Still, it's an unlikely scenario," Lucy continued. "If he was interested in taunting the police, he would have established contact before now. He likely sees me as a loose end—the one that got away and can give evidence that might lead police to him—or else as a challenge."

"Either way, you're a target," Bryce stated. He didn't like that scenario. She was still in danger because of him, because he'd asked her to come here. It was his duty, his responsibility to keep her safe. "I'll stay with you."

"I can take care of myself," she assured him, but he waved off her show of strength. She was in this mess because of him, and he had a duty to keep her safe. He owed it to her and to Danny, but most of all, he'd borne the responsibility of placing others in danger before, with terrible results. He wasn't sure he could go through that again.

"I'm not leaving."

She stared up at him, her eyes shining with gratitude and acceptance. "Okay, but only until I fall asleep. Then I insist you go home. The doctor will be releasing me in the morning. We'll go interview the floral shop employees then."

Ross nodded. "Great. Let me know what you find out." The forensics team signaled they were done, and Ross turned to leave. "I'm heading back out to the abduction site. I'll let you know if we find anything. I'll also have those files we talked about sent to the B&B."

"Thank you, Detective."

Bryce extended his hand and shook Ross's. "I appreciate all you're doing," he said, and he meant it. Ross hadn't had to go to bat for him with the chief and allow him to bring in the FBI, but he had and he was always fair enough to look at all the leads before making any conclusions. Bryce wished all the officers on the force showed the same restraint.

The nurse arrived and gave her something to help her pain, and Lucy seemed to rest better after that. Once she was sleeping soundly, Bryce slipped from the room and took up guard duty outside her door.

He passed the time by continuing to try to reach his brother and looking up the details of Danny's death. Something about the expression on Lucy's face when she'd told him about the car crash had left him wondering. He was sure she'd been hesitating, holding something back, and he feared the worst as he scoured the internet for news about the crash that had killed Danny and a family in a van.

He found articles on the crash from the previous year. A family of four, including two children, were killed when another driver had barreled through a traffic light and crashed into them. The driver of the car was also killed, and found to be under the influence of prescription medication at the time of the crash.

So that was what she hadn't wanted to tell him. Danny had been abusing prescription meds. Bryce sighed and rubbed a hand over his face as weariness weighed heavily on him. He'd known too many men, good men, who'd succumbed to addiction after suffering injuries in the service. As far as he'd known, Danny's injuries during his last combat mission hadn't been severe, certainly nothing that would have prevented him from returning after recovery. But he'd decided it was time to leave military life and focus on a career in law. The last time Bryce had spoken to Danny, he'd been excited about graduating law school and being hired by a criminal defense firm. He'd also been excited about planning a life with Lucy.

How easily it had all faded away.

He clicked on an image on his phone of him and Meghan taken only a few days after he'd returned home from his last mission as an SOA operator. It had been a rescue mission at an embassy and people had died, people he'd sent in to help the embassy workers. In an instant, his decision had cost three families their husbands, fathers, sons and brothers. It was a burden he had to live with, and one he didn't shoulder lightly.

He would look after Lucy because he owed it to her for the danger he'd placed her in. But he had to be careful too. He recalled how enamored Meghan had been with the lovely brunette FBI agent. She'd already texted him twice since he'd left her at her friend's house to check on her, and that was only after gushing about Lucy to her friend for several minutes after she'd arrived.

Yes, Lucy was turning out to be a fierce, amazingly strong federal agent, but that was all she could ever be in their lives. The press had called his SOA team heroes for acting to save lives, but his own government had labeled him insubordinate for not obeying their command to stand down and ignore the tragedy unfolding at the embassy. Lucy was a government agent, and Bryce had learned the hard way that his government could not be trusted—therefore Lucy could not be trusted.

No matter how her eyes seemed to twinkle at him.

TWO

Bryce arrived at the hospital the next morning carrying a suitcase. "I stopped by the B&B and asked Mrs. Ferguson to pack you some clothes from your room. I hope that's okay."

It was more than okay. It was wonderful, and Lucy was grateful he'd thought of it. She slipped from the hospital gown into a pair of jeans and a blouse and was finally starting to feel like a person again. She stared at herself in the mirror and saw a stranger staring back at her. The big ugly bruise took up one side of her face, and a busted lip completed the look.

The beating had been severe, and it was a blessing she hadn't sustained more than a mild concussion. Thinking about what might have been had been enough to keep her awake all night. Even now it made her stomach roll. She'd come to town to catch a killer, not to become his next victim.

"Thank you for the clothes," she told Bryce as she emerged from the bathroom where she'd changed. Last night the police had confiscated her running shoes for evidence, but Mrs. Ferguson had remembered to include another pair in the bag. She slipped them on, grimacing at the action. Her entire body ached from her ordeal, and she noticed Bryce didn't miss her grunts of pain.

"Are you sure you shouldn't be staying here?" he asked her.

She waved off his concerns. "I'm fine. Just a little sore. Getting out and moving will certainly help." That and the massive bottle of Tylenol she planned to keep with her at all times. The doctor had prescribed her painkillers, but she was hesitant to use them unless absolutely necessary. She wanted to be as alert as possible, and she'd tried to avoid strong painkillers ever since discovering Danny's addiction to them.

Bryce helped her slip into her jacket, and she couldn't help but notice the way his shoulders seemed to take up all her space, yet his hands were gentle as he helped her. It was strange to her that ever since hearing his daughter tell her that she would be okay because her dad was a marine, she had felt safer whenever he was around.

She shook off those feelings. She'd come here for a purpose, and it wasn't to cozy up to Bryce Tippitt. She couldn't even think about such things, not after what she'd been through with Danny. She had to keep her head about her and not get lulled into a sense of comfort. For all she knew, Bryce knew his brother was guilty and was grasping at straws to pin his crimes on another man. It was essential that she maintain her objectivity.

"I think we should head to the floral shop first," she said. She'd jotted down the name of the shop that bore the logo on the threatening note. "It was Busy Bee Flowers. Are you familiar with that shop?"

"Of course. I know right where it is."

"Good. Let's go then."

She was glad to get out of the hospital and ready to stop feeling like such an invalid. Wearing normal clothes certainly helped, but working out the kinks in her joints would make her feel better too.

The hospital insisted on forcing her to use a wheelchair until they reached the front doors. She hated it—one more reason she was glad to get out of there.

"I've already driven my pickup to the front doors," Bryce said as he wheeled her toward them. "A buddy of mine was able to replace the shattered back glass first thing this morning." He stopped abruptly.

"What's the matter?" she asked, glancing at the front doors. A group of people stood on the front stoop, blocking the path between the door and his truck. She spotted several cameras and knew they were the press. "What should we do?"

"We can find another way out, but I'll have to get my truck sometime."

"I can't ignore them forever. Let's just go through them. Let them have their photo op."

He nodded and pushed her toward the door. Once it slid open, the group turned and started snapping photos. Microphones were pushed into her face, and people shouted questions at her.

She ignored them, keeping her head down as Bryce opened the passenger door to his truck and helped her inside, leaving the wheelchair on the sidewalk. She was grateful for his calm manner and the hand on her back to keep her steady. She'd thought she could handle this, but the flashes of light and the shouting were unbearable. She was thankful when he slammed the door shut.

She covered her face as he walked around, climbed into the driver's seat and took off.

It was all too reminiscent of the days after Danny's death and the constant harassment by the press for a comment. She didn't know what they'd expected her to say. Nothing she could have said would have changed anything or brought any of them back to life.

The drive to the flower shop gave her enough time to pull herself together. Once they arrived, Bryce walked around and helped her out. He kept his distance enough to give her some sense of dignity, but he didn't stay so far away he couldn't help her if she stumbled. She recognized that and appreciated it.

She stepped into the shop and was immediately hit with the scent of flowers. Her eyes began to water as her allergies kicked in. This was going to be a quick interview, or else they were going to have to go into the back room.

She pulled out her FBI credentials and showed them to the clerk on duty. "I'd like to ask you some questions about a delivery that was made to Whitten Medical Center last night."

The woman behind the counter was in her forties with short hair and soft eyes. "Of course. I'm the owner, Charlotte Manchester. We had several deliveries there last night for the woman who escaped the serial killer. That was something special. That was you, wasn't it? Everyone who came in was excited that finally someone can identify him. It's what we've all been waiting for."

Lucy smiled at her, thankful for her kind sentiments. She hated to tell her that she couldn't identify him, that it had all happened so fast and that her attacker's face was nothing more than a blur in her mind. So she wouldn't tell her that. If the police wanted that information released, they would be the ones to do so. It wasn't smart to let the killer know she couldn't identify him, although it might take her out of his sights.

"That was me." There was no point in denying it. Her face would be all over the news in a matter of hours after the show while leaving the hospital. Plus how many FBI agents would be in town looking like they'd just gone several rounds in the boxing ring? "I received several very nice bouquets. The one I'm interested in came with this note." She pulled out a copy of the card Detective Ross had given her.

The woman read it and her face paled. "Oh my. That's terrible."

"Do you recall who wrote that?"

"No. Most of our orders were placed over the phone or online, but we did have several people walk in yesterday evening to purchase flowers. We were unusually busy last night. The entire town was excited about your escape. It had to be one of them, otherwise someone here would have written the card and I don't recognize this handwriting."

"But you don't know who that person was?"

"No. I wouldn't have sent it out knowing the note said something like that."

"Okay, what about receipts. Did anyone who came in pay with a credit card?"

"Yes, I have those records, although we had several people pay in cash. They're more likely to pay with cash if they come into the store."

"I'd like to see those receipts. I'd also like to know who else worked last night."

"I only have two other employees who help me. They both work part-time. I'll get you their names. And I'll copy that list for you." She disappeared into the back room.

"What do you think?" Bryce asked her.

"I think it's a dead end. I doubt someone who wrote that on a card would pay with a credit card, but we still have to check it out. Maybe Detective Ross will find a fingerprint to identify him."

"Do you really think the person who attacked you walked in here and purchased flowers for you? Wouldn't he be worried about being seen?"

Most people would think that, but Lucy knew from her experience that serial killers had a different mindset than most regular people. "Serial killers are known for being able to blend into society. It's why so many of them get away with it for so long."

Mrs. Manchester returned with the list. Lucy thanked her for her help and turned to leave, when the woman stopped her with a question. "You can identify him, can't you, Agent Sanderson? Please tell me this nightmare is over and you know who the killer is. It will put a lot of people at rest to know."

She glanced at Bryce, and Lucy knew she was anxious to hear if Clint Tippitt had been the one behind her attack. She saw Bryce flush with embarrassment. "I really can't say," Lucy told the woman. "It's still an ongoing investigation." She held up the paper. "Thank you for your help though, and have a nice day."

She and Bryce walked back outside to his truck, and

he helped her inside. Despite her blustering to Detective Ross yesterday about her ability to interview and interrogate witnesses, she was glad this venture hadn't called for that. She was tired and in more pain today than she had been yesterday. Her ankle was already protesting the short walk, and her head was pounding.

Bryce must have noticed because he suggested returning to the B&B. "I saw some boxes when I was there earlier, probably the ones Jim Ross sent over about the case."

He was giving her a way out of her posturing. Once again, she owed him. "You're right. I really should focus my attention on the cases. If I'm going to identify this killer, the clues will be in those files."

Bryce drove Lucy to the B&B where Mrs. Ferguson, an elderly lady with a lot of spunk and a big smile, greeted them at the door and gushed over Lucy.

"I heard what happened. How terrible for you, Lucy. Are you okay, dear?"

"Thank you, Mrs. Ferguson. I'm fine. Thank you for packing me some clothes. I also got your flowers last night. Sadly, the police had to confiscate all of them."

"What on earth for?"

Bryce set down her bag by the staircase. "It was a precaution. Someone sent Lucy a threatening message using flowers."

"How strange," the woman stated. "Two police officers brought by some boxes for you. They said they were files you requested. I had them leave them down here in the dining room. You're welcome to use the table if you need the room to go through them."

Lucy looked over and saw six boxes sitting in the

corner of the dining room. The table would provide her more room, but she didn't think anyone would care for graphic images of murdered women lying around. "That's kind of you, Mrs. Ferguson, but some of the images may be disturbing. You don't want them displayed in here."

"Well, it's only you and me here. I don't have any other guests right now, and I promise not to look. There's also a den in the back of the house. It has doors so you can close off the room. You're welcome to use that if you'd rather."

Lucy thanked her again and finally agreed to use the back room. With Bryce's help, she unloaded the files from their boxes, stacked them into appropriate piles and taped up photos of the victims, turning nearly one entire wall into an evidence wall.

She stared at the images of the victims. Her body ached from the attack and she wasn't at her best, but she had work to do and she was anxious to get to it.

She had a killer to catch.

Bryce helped Lucy unload the files, then spent the next several hours going through each case. The photos of the murdered women made his stomach roll. The thought that anyone could inflict such violence on another person angered and disgusted him. Yes, he'd seen violence. He'd even participated in it when necessary, but the face-to-face destruction of another person sickened him.

And to think his brother was being accused of these crimes.

"The last three victims all share the same modus

operandi. They were all abducted, missing for several days, then found with their throats slashed." Lucy picked up the photo of Jessica Nelson, the first victim, and his brother Clint's girlfriend at the time of her disappearance. "Jessica's case is different. It took place nearly two years before the next victim, and her body was never found."

"You don't think it's related?"

"Physically, it's impossible to link it to the other victims because she was never found. Her car is missing while the others were on foot when they were abducted, including myself, or else their car was found abandoned. I'll have to profile the victims to see if there's any overlap of their lives. I may be able to link them that way."

Lucy scanned through Jessica's case. "According to the report, she left Clint's house in her car headed home around 1:00 a.m. but never made it. Her body was never found, and neither was her car or any of her personal belongings." She glanced at Bryce. "Did you know her?"

"I did, although I wasn't around when she went missing. I was working overseas at the time."

"What was their relationship like?"

"Stormy. They fought a lot." Bryce knew his brother had loved Jessica and couldn't imagine him ever hurting her, but their relationship had never been a healthy one. Jealousy, drugs and alcohol had made for a bad mix between them.

"In the report, Clint says no one could confirm she really left that night. He was living alone at the time."

"Yes, he was."

"Where was Meghan? Where was she staying?"

"With her mother. That was before she died."

Lucy gasped. "I'm sorry. I wasn't aware you were widowed."

Her sympathy was appreciated but unnecessary. "Actually, we never married. We dated in high school, then I joined the military. I only learned years later that Bridgette had given birth to Meghan and hadn't told me. I spent the next several years fighting for my rights in court just to see her."

"She kept Meghan from you?"

It had been a difficult time in his life, a time when he'd believed everyone and everything was against him. "She did. My family wasn't exactly known to be upstanding members of the community. Bridgette and her parents fought to keep Meghan from me. In fact, if Cassidy hadn't written to me telling me about her, I might not have ever known I had a daughter."

"Cassidy? That was your friend at the hospital?"

"Yes. We grew up together before her folks moved out of town when she was ten. She came back to live with her grandparents and finish high school, and we became friends again. She was probably the only friend I had growing up." He didn't know why he was opening up to Lucy this way. He had friends in the military who never knew about his struggles. He was used to keeping things to himself, but something about Lucy made him want to open up and know that he wouldn't be judged.

"We didn't have an easy childhood and, I'm sorry to say, I got into a lot of trouble growing up. After my dad died, my mom worked three jobs to keep a roof over our heads and food on the table, but that also meant she wasn't around much."

"That sounds like a lonely way to live."

"I guess it's true what they say about negative attention being better than no attention. I made sure I received plenty of negative attention. Clint followed every move I made…except when it came to joining the military. He wanted nothing to do with it. Instead, he got into drugs and stealing cars and ended up spending three years in prison, all while I was overseas."

She reached over and covered his hand with hers. "Well, it looks like you're doing well enough now. Meghan is a wonderful girl, and I'm sure that's your influence. You said her mother died?"

"She died in a car crash three years ago. After that, I was able to get sole custody and I worked out a deal with her grandparents. She would stay with them while I was on assignment, and they wouldn't interfere any longer with my relationship with my daughter. It's worked out well so far. Only, I'm not sure what will happen now. I don't know if I'm going back overseas."

"Because of your brother?"

"No. I've been working covert security overseas. A few months ago, my unit was involved in a rescue mission of an American embassy. We were ordered to stand down, but we went in anyway."

"I heard about that incident. According to the news, you're all heroes."

"Well, according to the federal government, we disobeyed orders. Especially now that there's been so much media coverage about it, I doubt the agency will be offering me another contract assignment." He surprised himself sharing so much with her. Usually, he was closemouthed about his life and his feelings, but something about Lucy engendered trust in him.

He shook his head, trying to remember that she was part of the government and therefore part of the problem. He'd been burned too many times before, and besides, her hand on his was just a little too appealing to him.

"I should go now," he said, standing. "It's getting late and Meghan will be waiting for me."

He didn't want to go or leave Lucy, and that bothered him too. He'd grown protective of her in a short time, but he had responsibilities to his daughter too.

"Good night," he said as he walked out.

He had to keep his emotions under control. Lucy was only here to do a job. Prove his brother innocent—and Bryce wasn't going to do anything that would jeopardize that.

Lucy yawned and decided to call it a night. She stacked up the files and placed them back into the boxes, wishing she'd asked Bryce to carry them upstairs for her. She could at least take a few files in case she couldn't sleep, so she wouldn't have to come back downstairs and disturb Mrs. Ferguson.

The older lady stopped her before she went upstairs. "Is Bryce gone? I was going to offer him some of this lasagna we had for supper to take home to Meghan."

"I'm sure he'll be sorry. He just left. It was delicious, by the way. You shouldn't have gone to so much trouble."

"Nonsense. Why do you think I opened this bed-and-breakfast? I enjoy taking care of people. I'll put the remainder in the refrigerator in case you want some more later."

"Thank you, Mrs. Ferguson, but I think this day is catching up to me. I'm going to take a shower then turn in for the night."

"Rest well, Lucy. I'm going to finish cleaning up the kitchen then turn in myself. See you in the morning."

Lucy walked upstairs. She was tired through and through, but at least today she felt like she'd accomplished something. The flower shop was more than likely a dead end for information about the threatening note, but learning more about the murdered women had helped her get a grip on what was going on in this town.

She knew now why Bryce had reached out to her. It was obvious the police were focusing all their attention on his brother because of his relationship with the missing girl, but after examining all the evidence, she couldn't find anything to link her disappearance with the murdered women.

She was glad she was here. She was glad to still be able to help people by identifying a killer and aiding in bringing safety back to a community. So kids like Meghan didn't have to be afraid to go out with her friends.

Why was she thinking about Meghan? Sure, it was for the girl's sake, but she felt it had more to do with Meghan's blue-eyed, former marine father and the way his touch had sent sparks through her. But how would Bryce Tippitt feel if her profile didn't exonerate his brother as the killer? If it gave the local police more leverage against him? She couldn't worry about that. Her job was to create a behavioral profile based on the evidence collected from each of the crime scenes and victim etiology. And she was good at her job. Or she had been before Danny anyway, before her confidence had taken a nosedive. She couldn't let someone else, another man no less, disrupt her concentration because she was mildly attracted to his broad shoulders and warm smile.

Stop it, she told herself. She couldn't go there. Romance was out of the question. She didn't deserve a second chance at love, and she wasn't going to risk it again. She took a shower and changed into a pair of yoga pants and a T-shirt to sleep in.

Suddenly, a large crash from downstairs caught her attention.

Lucy grabbed her gun from the nightstand and hurried downstairs. She called out to Mrs. Ferguson. "Is everything all right?"

No answer. Not even the hum of the woman as she cleaned the dishes.

Lucy walked down the steps. The first night she'd arrived, before her run, the house had been filled with the sounds of Mrs. Ferguson humming as she did the dishes. Tonight, everything was quiet.

Lucy glanced at her watch. Mrs. Ferguson told her she was usually in her chair in front of the TV by this time every night. The television was still off. "Mrs. Ferguson? Is everything all right?"

She had a growing suspicion it was not. Her instincts were kicking in, but she tried to tell herself she was just hyperaware after being abducted, yet she couldn't shake off the eerie feeling that something wasn't right. How would she even know what was right or wrong in this house? It was only her second night here.

She approached the kitchen, hoping and praying she would push open the door to find Mrs. Ferguson humming quietly as she handwashed the dishes. No sense using the dishwasher, she'd said, for only two people.

She pushed open the door to the kitchen. It was empty. Hairs were standing up on her neck, a sign that something was seriously wrong. A flash at the window had her spinning around. Someone was there. Outside. She rushed to the door and down the back stoop, staring into the night with only the light from the streetlamp to illuminate the yard.

"Who's out there?" she demanded.

She stepped into the darkness and moved around the corner of the house. Another shadow flitted, and she hurried to catch up to it.

"FBI! Freeze!" she demanded, but she saw no one when she ran around the back corner. Her ankle was screaming for relief, and her head was beginning to pound. It had been such a long day. Perhaps her nerves were finally getting to her. She headed toward the back door, slamming into a figure as she turned the corner.

A scream lit up the night, and too late Lucy realized she'd knocked down Mrs. Ferguson. Lucy lunged to catch her, but only managed to trip and fall herself. She slammed onto the concrete pavers and rammed her knee into one.

"Mrs. Ferguson, I'm so sorry. Are you hurt?"

The older woman sat up and checked herself. "No, I'm surprisingly uninjured. I'm sorry, dear. You frightened me."

Lucy scrambled to her feet and helped Mrs. Ferguson up. "I was searching for you. I heard a noise and I was afraid something had happened to you."

"No, no. I received a call asking if I could walk Mrs.

Littleton's dog because she'd decided to stay another night at her sister's house. But Mrs. Littleton was at home. She hadn't even gone to her daughter's house. Why on earth would someone do that?"

Nothing about that sounded right. "You didn't recognize the voice?"

"No, but that's not unusual. I don't hear that well anymore. I assumed it was her daughter calling me. They have my number, and I'm always glad to help whenever they need me."

Lucy was certainly willing to believe Mrs. Ferguson was known for her helpfulness. "Perhaps you misunderstood the caller."

She nodded. "Yes, that must be it."

Suddenly a figure appeared in the darkness. "What's going on?"

Lucy spun around, gun raised and all her senses on alert.

Bryce raised his hands and backed up. "Whoa. It's only me."

"What are you doing back here?" she asked, her heart rate beginning to slow.

"Mrs. Ferguson called me earlier and said if I wasn't too far away, I should swing back and take home some of her lasagna for Meghan. I was at the gas station when she phoned."

"Yes, I did make that call," Mrs. Ferguson stated. "I'm glad I did. You're back just in the nick of time. Lucy thinks someone was in the house."

Bryce's composure shifted to protective mode. "Are you sure?"

She saw his concern and felt silly at her obvious misinterpretation. "No, I'm not."

"Let's check anyway."

He headed inside, and Lucy instructed Mrs. Ferguson to wait while they searched the house. She and Bryce looked through every room and saw no evidence of an intruder. Lucy was starting to feel like she'd imagined the threat—until she opened the door to the back room.

She shouted for Bryce, who was upstairs checking the bedrooms. She stared at the mess that was now her workspace. All her papers were strewn everywhere, and someone had been searching through her things. And on the wall, in freshly painted large letters, was a threat.

Leave town now or pay the price.

Bryce went through the entire house, checking all the doors and windows. He found what he was looking for in the first-floor living room. One of the back windows had been busted out, and it was obvious the intruder had gotten in that way. That must have been the noise Lucy had heard that made her investigate.

Lucy did her best to make Mrs. Ferguson comfortable while they waited for the police to arrive. He couldn't help but notice how gentle she was with the older woman, and it spoke of her kindness.

The police arrived and got busy dusting for fingerprints and taking Mrs. Ferguson's statement about the call she'd received that had lured her out of the house.

Bryce chatted with Jim Ross about the likelihood of finding the person who'd placed the fake call.

"We'll try to trace the call, but if the guy was smart, he used an untraceable burner. It's unlikely anything will come of it."

"At least he didn't try to harm her."

Ross nodded. "We'll increase patrols around her house just in case too."

"Thanks, Jim. I appreciate it."

Bryce looked for Lucy and found her in the back room glancing through her evidence files. The offending threat had already been photographed and well documented, but it sickened him to look at. He'd go by the hardware store tomorrow and pick up paint to cover it.

"What are you looking at?" he asked her.

"Just checking to see if anything was bothered."

"Was it?"

"Only this." She handed him a photo of Jessica Nelson, the same one they'd looked at earlier. Green paint now dotted its edges.

"He looked through the evidence."

"This is the only thing I can find with any paint on it. It's all he touched. I mean, why take the time to break in? What was he looking for? What did he want?"

He motioned toward the threat painted on the wall. "To do that, I suppose."

"It doesn't make sense, Bryce. The man who abducted me on the road—" she picked up the evidence photos of the murdered women "—the man who did this, he's a killer. He wouldn't be the type of person to orchestrate getting Mrs. Ferguson out of the house and vandalize my room just to frighten me into leaving town. It doesn't fit what we know about him. Why not snatch us both? Or kill her then come after me?"

"Serial killers have types, don't they? All of these women are between a certain age. Mrs. Ferguson is in her seventies. Maybe she didn't fit his type."

"Then he would have killed her and moved on. Besides, he brought the paint with him. He came here planning to do this with no intention of hurting anyone."

"Could this be his way of reaching out to you like you said about the note? Taunting you?"

"He has no history of doing that before." She shook her head, and worry clouded her expression. "It doesn't feel right." She sighed then turned to him. "I'd be remiss if I didn't ask this—do you know where your brother was an hour ago?"

He hated the suspicion he saw on her face. "I knew someone would be asking me that question." He hadn't expected it to be her. He'd brought her here to help his brother, not join the accusers. "The answer is no. I haven't seen him or spoken to him. But then again, there are a lot of people I haven't seen today either. You're only asking about Clint because they've put it in your head that he's involved in those women's deaths."

"No, I'm asking because the only photo he bothered was the one of Jessica Nelson. Why would anyone else be interested in it?"

He gave a resigned sigh. Bryce was tired of the constant questioning of his brother's motives, but she did have a point. "I don't know. But Clint would have no reason to threaten you. You came to town to help him."

"I also came here to profile a serial killer. Is it possible he's worried I'll uncover him in the process?"

He shook his head. "No. It's not. He didn't do this," he said, motioning toward the horrific photos of murdered women. "He couldn't have."

"Why are you so certain your brother didn't do this? It has to be more than family loyalty. You have to at least entertain the possibility. I can spout off countless instances where offenders were arrested for horrific crimes and their family members insisted they couldn't be responsible." She turned and rubbed her neck. "What is it about those we love that makes us doubt their culpability?"

He heard the weariness in her voice and wondered if she was thinking about Danny and the traffic accident. Had she known about his drug usage, or had she been as oblivious as she seemed to believe he was?

But her question had merit, and if he wanted her help, he needed to explain what must seem like crazy loyalty to his brother. "I've seen evil, Lucy. I've faced it down eye to eye." He shuddered at the memory of the men who'd attacked the embassy and their disregard for anyone's life. "There's a coldness in their eyes. I don't see that in my brother. I'm not saying he's perfect. He's messed up royally, I'll admit that, but he's no killer. He doesn't have it in him."

She looked like she was about to challenge him again, then she just sat down.

He took the seat beside her. "What are you thinking?"

"That someone wants me to leave town, but it's not the same person who abducted me yesterday or who killed all those women."

He had to agree with her assessment. Whoever heard

of a cold-blooded killer breaking into a house only to send a threatening message? A killer was going to kill until someone stopped him.

But someone was determined to frighten her into leaving town.

If it wasn't the killer then who was it? And why?

THREE

Lucy felt more like a person again after a good night's sleep and normal clothes, including her heels, which gave her a slight height advantage she enjoyed. She needed the boost of confidence today as she formally met with Chief Dobson and the task force.

After Bryce and the police had left and the house was quiet again, she'd spent the evening going back through the case files until sleep had finally forced her to give in.

She'd taken up the files again this morning over breakfast even as a freshly showered and shaved Bryce arrived in time to enjoy Mrs. Ferguson's breakfast spread, at her insistence of course.

"Did you ever contact your brother?"

A mournful look spread across his face. "I haven't. I've tried calling and texting with no response. He has a place on the outskirts of town he bought last year where he spends a lot of his time. It's an old warehouse he uses for woodworking. I'm going to swing by today to see if he's there. I can't imagine where else he would be."

Lucy hoped he was there. She was in town to defend

a man she hadn't even met. His brother was going out of his way to fight for his innocence, and it seemed to Lucy he couldn't even be bothered to show up. It seemed like it had been days since Bryce had first started trying to reach him, but she realized it had been only a day. Just one day since she'd been abducted, shot at and threatened.

The more she thought about the circumstances of both the threatening note and the break-in last night, the more she was convinced it was the work of someone other than the Back Roads Killer. It didn't fit with a serial killer's profile.

Bryce took her hands as he parked the truck in front of the police station. "Don't be nervous," he told her. "Chief Dobson is loud and obnoxious."

She waited for the "but," only none came. It was obvious he held no love for the man, and why would he? This was the guy who was trying to convict his brother of murder.

"Tell me how you really feel about Dobson."

He gave her a wry smile as he got out of his truck and walked around to her door. "He's allowing you to work with the task force, so I suppose I owe him for that." He helped her out, and she noticed his hands remained on her waist even once she was on her feet. She liked it.

"I'll be fine," she assured him. "This isn't the first time I've dealt with obnoxious and loud. I am an FBI agent after all. It comes with the job."

His lips curved into a smile, and it surprised her how much she liked it. She hadn't noticed a man's smile in a long time. Not since Danny.

"What are you doing with him?" a voice demanded from behind her.

Lucy turned to see a dark-haired woman with worry lines prominent around her eyes and mouth. "Excuse me?"

"Why are you talking to him? Aren't you the FBI agent everyone is talking about? You're supposed to be finding evidence to prove Clint Tippitt killed my daughter, not spending time with his brother."

She knew she was already news around town—given that reporters had been camped out under her hospital window—but Lucy hadn't expected to be confronted while walking in town. "I'm Agent Lucy Sanderson, but my job isn't to—"

"You have to make him tell you what he did with my daughter," the woman said, her fingers pressing deep into Lucy's arm. "My daughter Jessica was the first girl who went missing. You have to make that lowlife Clint Tippitt tell you what he did with her. It's been four years. I want to bury my daughter. Please."

Her pleas were desperate and sincere, and Lucy felt for her. If and when the time came to interrogate Clint, Lucy would come up with a behavioral profile to help the police ask questions that might get Clint to give up Jessica's whereabouts. "I'll do my best to find out what happened to your daughter, ma'am. Any way I can assist the police to close this case, I'll do it."

The woman pulled out a photo of Jessica with her family. "She was so young, Agent Sanderson. She didn't deserve what happened to her. I warned her about hanging out with that Tippitt boy. That whole family is no good."

Her face seemed to soften when she spoke about her daughter. Lucy couldn't imagine the pain she was going through knowing that someone had taken her child from her, but she could still feel the wash of guilt arise in her at knowing she'd played a part in taking the children and grandchildren from not one, but two sets of parents.

Mrs. Nelson's face hardened as she looked past Lucy, then rushed toward Bryce. "You! You stay away from this, Bryce. This has nothing to do with you."

"I'd say it does, Mrs. Nelson, if you're here to poison Agent Sanderson against my brother."

"He's a murderer!"

"There has never been any proof that Clint did anything to your daughter."

"He's a murderer like his father before him. You Tippitts are nothing but a family of murderers."

Lucy was surprised by that remark, and one look at the way Bryce reddened and avoided her gaze told her there was more to the story about his father.

She noticed Bryce's jaw tense and the way he slipped his hands into his pockets in an effort to keep control of his emotions as this lady spewed accusations at him. What was it like having such hatred gushing at you like that? And the way Mrs. Nelson was lunging at him, Lucy suspected she was close to lashing out physically.

"Stop it," Lucy told them both, getting between them. "Stop it. Mrs. Nelson, I assure you I will do everything I can to find out what happened to your daughter, but blaming Bryce for something his brother might have done will get you nowhere."

Mrs. Nelson shrank at Lucy's words. "So it's Bryce now, is it? I see he's already reeled you into his web of lies. That's what they do, Agent Sanderson. They're all liars and killers." She grabbed Lucy's arm again and dug in. "Don't fall for their lies. Don't let them win."

Lucy pulled her arm away. "Mrs. Nelson, please calm down. You're being unreasonable."

She stalked away, and Bryce had the good sense to step away too and take several deep breaths.

"She really believes your brother did something to her daughter."

"Chief Dobson has convinced her that Clint was involved, and she refuses to hear anything else. I don't guess he had to try hard to convince her. Clint was always the main suspect in her disappearance."

She studied him. Since she'd arrived in town, he'd been a pillar of strength and courage, but now he shrank from her. "What did she mean when she said Clint was like his father?"

"It's nothing. Only gossip and rumors."

"I'd like to be the judge of that."

"What does it have to do with any of this? It has no bearing on whether or not Clint killed those women, does it?"

He was right. Knowing something terrible about his father shouldn't change the facts of the case. And her profile was based on facts, not on something that happened in a suspect's childhood. But a killer's childhood could play a role in his psychology...if Clint was the killer. But she could see Bryce wasn't ready to share that story, and she wasn't going to push him for it yet. "I'm sorry. You're right. Rumors don't matter. I'll see you in a bit, okay?"

She turned to walk toward the police precinct, but his next words stopped her.

"When I was eleven, my father was accused of killing a woman in our church he'd been having an affair with."

It seemed he'd decided it did matter. She turned back to him and saw the pain those words, and that memory, caused him. His jaw was set in anger, but his face was red with shame. "Was he convicted?"

He shook his head. "He shot himself before the case ever went to trial. He left a note saying he couldn't live with how he'd hurt his family. In this town, taking his own life was as good as a confession."

The angst in his expression was enough to make Lucy's heart break. He was a good man who was fighting so hard for his family. And he was right. Knowing about his father's past deeds shouldn't alter her profile, but it certainly had to alter people's opinions. "I'm sorry."

"I figure someone would have told you before the day was out, so I'd better go ahead and say it first." He shook his head in disgust. "I told you the members of my family weren't exactly upstanding citizens."

She doubted anyone felt that way about Bryce.

He leaned against his truck. "I'll be waiting here for you…if you still want me to."

She wouldn't give him the option of self-pity. Besides, she still felt more comfortable with him by her side, and this news didn't change that.

She moved close to him, leaning in, then placed a kiss on his cheek, surprising even herself by the bold move. "I'll see you soon," she said, hoping to reassure him that she was still on his side. But her knees quivered as she walked away, and it had nothing to do with the beating she'd received and everything to do with the man she'd just kissed.

She headed inside and asked the receptionist to let Detective Ross know she was here. Minutes later he appeared and led her into the chief's office. Chief Charles Dobson was a large man with a presence that filled the room even as he sat behind his desk. Lucy stood up straighter. He struck her as the kind of man who commanded respect from those who worked with him.

He introduced himself to Lucy. "You're the FBI profiler we were expecting?"

"That's right."

"Well, it seems you've already met the man we wanted you to profile. That's not FBI protocol to get abducted by the killer you're profiling, is it?"

She felt her face redden as embarrassment rushed through her. "No, it's not." But she wasn't going to let the Whitten Police Department be dissuaded from utilizing her skills because of this awful incident. "But it does give us an advantage."

"How is that? I heard you weren't able to identify the man who attacked you."

"I never saw his face."

"Great. Our only living witness, and you know nothing." His dismissive tone rankled her. Did he always speak to victims in such a manner? "I didn't say I had nothing. I may not have seen his face, but I can still be a witness. I was able to give your task force valuable information such as the attacker's approximate size and weight, where he attacked and what his method of abduction was. I can tell you where I was abducted from and what area of town I was in when I escaped so you can begin a search for a hideout of some kind. He tried to drug me with a needle to my neck, which means he uses some form of drugs to incapacitate his victims."

He looked at her and grinned, his interest obviously piqued. "Okay, you got me. You're a witness. The task force processed the scene where he abducted you yesterday. We'll go over the preliminary reports during the meeting. Anything else you've remembered that might be of help?"

"No, Chief. I've shared everything I remember with Detective Ross."

He nodded. "Do you want me to call anyone from the FBI for you? Do they need to send someone else down here?"

"That won't be necessary. I'm still able to do my job. This is only a sprained ankle and some cuts and bruises. I'm perfectly capable of continuing on."

"Good. Now let's talk about these threats you've received." He turned to Ross. "Do we have any leads on those?"

"No, we don't, Chief. The card from the flower shop had only Lucy's fingerprints, plus the nurse from the hospital and Jake Gibbons, a college-aged worker at the store. We have those on file from a DUI. That's his only offense on record."

"What about the break-in at the Ferguson home?"

"Fingerprinting hasn't turned up anything there either, and we've canvassed the neighborhood. Several people reported seeing someone running from the house, but no one could describe him. It was too dark."

He thought about it and rubbed his face, then turned

to Lucy. "What's your take on these threats, Agent Sanderson? If this guy is targeting you—"

"I don't believe that's the case, Chief. I don't believe the threats are coming from the killer."

"So you arrive in town, are abducted by a serial killer, then receive threats telling you to leave town and you don't think they're related?"

"I don't. It doesn't fit the profile of this killer. It's my understanding that so far he's shown no interest in connecting with law enforcement, and the behavior we're witnessing—leaving threats and luring Mrs. Ferguson from the home, for instance, so she won't be hurt—indicate someone who doesn't like the one-on-one intimacy that are trademarks of these murders. The person behind these threats doesn't enjoy getting his hands dirty the same way our serial killer does. He thrives on it, and I believe if he were responsible for these threats, Mrs. Ferguson would be dead and so would I. He wouldn't be threatening me so I'd leave town."

"Well, who else would do this?"

She'd actually given that a lot of thought. "Anyone who doesn't want or appreciate FBI interference in this case. Perhaps someone who wants the glory of finding this killer for himself or his precinct." It wouldn't be the first time she'd witnessed hostility from local law enforcement about the FBI coming in on a case, but it would be the first time it had gone to the extreme of trying to threaten an agent into leaving town.

Chief Dobson stood and stared at her hard. She'd expected as much. She'd accused someone in his department of being behind the threats against her. "Are you suggesting one of my people is responsible?"

"I'm only surmising. It could actually be anyone in town with a grudge against the FBI." She needed to contact her supervisor and find out if anyone in town was under FBI investigation or showed up on their radar.

But Chief Dobson was having none of her speculation. "Isn't it possible you brought this threat to town with you? Someone from one of your old cases perhaps?"

She couldn't think of anyone who had a problem with her besides someone who might be angry over Danny's actions, or the extended members of the Williams family, relatives of those who'd died in the van. But why attack now, half a continent away and a year later? That made no sense. And she hadn't worked any high-profile cases since before Danny's death that would cause anyone to want to harm her. "It's unlikely. This threat has to be coming from someone in Whitten since they apparently want me to leave town." But just to be safe, she would also have someone go through her previous case files to see if anyone she'd had a hand in convicting had recently been released or was living in the area.

Another officer knocked on the office door, then stuck his head in. "We're ready for you, Chief."

Chief Dobson stood. "We'll keep increased patrols on the Ferguson B&B for now, but unless another threat occurs, our focus needs to remain on the killer."

"I agree," Lucy told him. She also wanted to know who was behind the threats, but so far, no real damage had been done. Bryce had promised to come by the Ferguson home and paint over the offending threat later today. A killer on the loose had to take precedence.

Lucy followed the chief and Detective Ross to a conference room where several officers sat around a large table. She limped to her seat, acutely aware that she'd already been damaged in the eyes of this police force. She was no longer the professional tough-as-nails FBI profiler she imagined they'd been expecting. She was now a victim of the very killer she'd been sent here to find.

It hurt, knowing their opinions of her were already tainted. She'd been hoping for a clean, fresh start with this case, another opportunity to prove she was still that capable agent she'd been before Danny's death. But their opinions of her couldn't distract her from doing her job.

She listened as Detective Ross updated the task force on the evidence they'd collected from her crime scene. "We located a full syringe, which Agent Sanderson claims the assailant tried to inject her with. We're sending the contents of the syringe to the lab for processing, but we surmise it was some sort of sedative."

Lucy spoke up. "Based on the way he blitz attacked me, I'm guessing he used the sedative to incapacitate his victims, then placed them in his trunk for transporting the way he did with me."

"That would have been easy for him given that, like you, Agent Sanderson, two of the remaining victims were on foot when they were abducted."

Lucy dug through her files for the reports on twenty-two-year-old Ashley Carlton, who'd been abducted while walking home at night from a convenience store, and fourteen-year-old Kimberly Wren, who'd sneaked out of her house at night to meet a friend. Both females were found beaten, raped and murdered days after their abductions.

The other victim, sixteen-year-old Presley Oliver,

had vanished while driving home from a football game. "Is it possible she had car trouble or he pushed her off the road?" Lucy asked.

Ross shook his head. "Our techs went over her car. They found nothing wrong with it."

"Then he found a way to lure her out of it." If they could uncover some tactic he used, such as pretending to be a police officer in order to get her to pull to the side of the road, that would be an important aspect of the case to focus on. But he hadn't used any tactics like that on Lucy. He'd simply attacked her. "Have there been reports of anyone approaching women pretending to be police officers or someone using a ruse to get women to pull their cars over to the side of the road?"

Ross glanced at the other officers, who all shook their heads. "Not that we're aware of."

"It wouldn't hurt to ask for the public's help in reporting any such incidents. There may be women he approached who never pulled over so he moved on. If it worked on this victim, it's possible he's tried it again."

Chief Dobson spoke up. "Let's have the Public Information Officer put out a request for anyone who's witnessed this happening to call us and report it. We should be able to get the request on the news at noon."

"Anything else?" Ross asked her.

"Yes." She referred to the case files again. "He's increasing the amount of time he spends with each of his victims. Presley Oliver was found three days later, while Ashley and Kimberly were found five and six days, respectively, after they were abducted. This shows he's comfortable holding these women for long periods of time. He must have a secure place to keep them, somewhere they can't escape and where no one can hear them or interrupt him."

"That could be almost anywhere," one of the officers stated.

"True, but it's an important detail to keep in mind as leads come in. Before I managed to jump from the trunk of his car, the suspect turned off from the main road onto a dirt road heading into the woods. He had to be going somewhere."

Ross pulled up a map on the screen and pointed to an area. "This is where Bryce said he found Agent Sanderson wandering on the road." He circled an area. "If he turned off the main road, he was likely heading into the woods. This area is mostly used as hunting grounds. Let's start a search of the area for any place he could be holding these women. Sheds, trailers, campers—check anything you can find."

Ross's idea for the search seemed solid and Lucy hoped it would turn up something, but even from the map on the screen, she could see that the area was massive. She still had to continue with her profile. "I'd like to know more about the first victim, Jessica Nelson. What made you tie her disappearance to the other murders? There doesn't seem to be much in common with the other cases."

"We were already investigating the Nelson case. When another woman went missing, it seemed logical to assume they were connected."

"Okay, but at some point you had to see there was very little evidence to connect her case with the others. For starters, there's a two-year span of time between when she disappeared and when the next victim was abducted. And only months between the subsequent abduction and murders. Plus the bodies of the other victims were found. We know what happened to them."

"Her parents have come to terms with the fact that she was killed—" one of the officers began.

"And why do they believe that?" Lucy interrupted. "Because you do? Because you've painted the scenario around town that Clint Tippitt killed her in an act of rage and disposed of both her body and her car so well that neither have ever been found despite exhaustive efforts by this police force? What you've spread is conjecture." She saw by the looks of surprise on their faces that they weren't used to being contradicted. What kind of task force wasn't open to new ideas?

"We haven't spread anything, Agent Sanderson. But when the next girl went missing then turned up dead, people quickly came to their own assumptions."

"There's no evidence of that," Lucy interjected. He and everyone else looked her way. Clearly they'd already concluded that Jessica Nelson was dead. "I understand your department's assumptions, but there's no proof that she's dead. She should still be classified as a missing person."

Chief Dobson stood and folded his arms. His expression mimicked those of his officers. They didn't like her assessment, and they didn't agree with it.

"I know you've been through something, Agent Sanderson. That wasn't the best introduction to our little town. I also know you're grateful to Bryce Tippitt for his assistance to you and the fact that he brought you in. I do hope you won't let that color your judgment on this matter."

He was heading right where she'd been fearful he would go. After all, she was now pretty certain they wanted this profile to help implicate Clint Tippitt in these murders, and were only interested in leads that directed them toward that goal. They had little else in the way of evidence to implicate him in the other murders. With three dead girls, they were looking for someone to pay for the crimes.

But she wasn't in the business of creating profiles to help with prosecution. Her profiles were meant to help identify offenders and, in this case, she wasn't yet convinced of Clint Tippitt's involvement in the murders. Yet he wasn't wrong about her being able to maintain objectivity. Her face burned with embarrassment, recalling how she'd kissed Bryce earlier. How was that remaining objective?

She stared at the chief and put on her best professional demeanor. "This isn't my first trip out of the academy, Chief. I've worked on several high-profile cases, and I can assure you the profile I create will in no way reflect any personal preference. I'm about the science of behavioral analysis, nothing else." She paused. That wasn't exactly true. "I will be including my own abduction experience to see if it lines up at all with the other cases, but that will be the extent of my personal investment."

He wouldn't be wrong in suggesting she call someone else in to complete this profile, but she was going to attempt to steer him away from doing so. She was here now, and this had turned personal. This offender had targeted her, attacked her, abducted her. She was going to do her best to separate the emotional response to her ordeal from the cold, hard facts, but they were in uncharted territory when it came to the events she'd experienced. They had no way of knowing how these victims had been lured in by their attacker, only her experience of being grabbed to assume that was his modus operandi. He'd meant her harm, and she figured it was safe to assume there wasn't more than one homicidal maniac roaming around this town.

The chief glanced at his cell phone, then addressed the room before ending the meeting. "I've been informed that Clint Tippitt presented himself to the emergency room early this morning needing stitches for a cut on his right arm—the same arm Agent Sanderson claimed she scratched."

A gasp went through the room, and Lucy felt her own breath catch. She'd advised everyone to be watching for someone showing up with a bandage or arm wound, but she'd never expected this turn of events.

"I'm sending a patrol car to pick him up for questioning in Agent Sanderson's abduction."

"I'm sure I didn't scratch him severely enough to need stitches," Lucy said.

"According to the charge nurse, he claimed his injury was the result of a table saw wound. It's possible he cut himself with the saw to cover up the scratch you gave him." It made little sense to her that someone would do that to cover up a scratch, but Chief Dobson seemed sure of himself. "We're also going to have the forensics team go through his car for evidence." He glanced at Lucy. "It's possible that it's the same car you spent some time in."

Chief Dobson headed out, but Lucy stopped to gather

her thoughts. This should have been a good turn of events, but her only thought was how devastating this news would be to Bryce.

Bryce used the time Lucy was meeting with the task force to try to track down his brother. It had already been over thirty-six hours since he'd last spoken to or heard from Clint.

He headed to the main highway out of town. Clint had bought a structure that used to be a storage building. He'd fixed it up with woodworking materials to pursue his carpentry hobby, and even though he had a room at the ranch, he spent most of his days and nights there. He'd always been good with his hands, and could probably make a decent living at it if he really tried.

Bryce pushed back those kinds of thoughts. They were counterproductive. He hated seeing his little brother with no ambition and no clear definition of what he wanted from life. He was nearing thirty and still seemed to be drifting.

He checked that attitude as well since he himself didn't have a clear idea of where his own life was heading now that his career with SOA was probably over. What was he supposed to do next? Rejoin the marines? Private security? Stay home and build his ranch? On some level, staying in Whitten appealed to him, but he was certain he would get bored quickly. He wasn't the type to sit around and do nothing. He needed a purpose and a mission.

He tried Clint's phone again, and again it went to voice mail. Where was he? He prayed his brother was out with a group of people who could vouch that he'd been nowhere near the highway when Agent Lucy Sanderson was abducted.

But even as he lifted that silent prayer toward heaven, he knew it was unlikely. His brother had grown into more of an introvert over the years since his girlfriend, Jessica, had gone missing and was presumed murdered. He preferred to spend his time alone. He didn't have many friends, and that was in part because of the police, who continued to name him a killer.

Lord, I know Lucy came to town to find a killer, but could You please also help her find proof of Clint's innocence?

She had the killer's DNA. That would certainly put to rest any rumors about his involvement, but those results were weeks away and any number of things could happen before then. The local cops were fired up to bring down his brother in their desire to stop a killer. He hoped Lucy would be more open-minded in her investigation.

He pulled into the parking area around the building and got out. Clint's car was in a space nearby, and Bryce heard music blaring from inside. At least he knew he was there. He knocked but was sure his brother couldn't hear him over the music. He checked the side door and found it unlocked, so he entered.

Clint was standing at his table saw working. Bryce picked up his brother's phone, the source of the blaring music, and turned down the volume. Clint finally noticed him, then turned off the saw. "What are you doing here?"

"I've been trying to call you. Why haven't you picked up?" He tossed Clint his phone and his brother glanced at the screen, obviously noting an abundance of missed calls and texts.

"I've been busy. And I'm not used to having to report in with you. I got along just fine when you were gone, remember?"

Bryce grimaced. He did remember, and he felt guilty for not being around for Clint, but he'd had his own life to live. And it was obvious to Bryce his brother had been ignoring his calls and messages. "Multiple arrests plus suspicion of murder? I wouldn't call that fine."

He didn't mean to sound like a parent, but Clint's face hardened. "I'm an adult, aren't I? I don't have to answer to you, Bryce. I needed some time alone."

"I didn't mean to pry. It's just—"

Clint slipped off his jacket, revealing a bandage on his arm sticking out from beneath a tear on his shirt.

He zeroed in on that bandage and recalled Lucy saying she'd scratched her attacker on the right arm. "Wh-what happened to your arm?"

Clint shrugged it off. "I cut myself with a table saw while I was woodworking last night."

This did not look good for his brother. A moment of doubt filled him. He didn't really believe his brother was capable of murder. But how could he ignore the signs?

"I haven't seen or spoken to you for over a day. Are you saying you've been here that entire time? Alone?"

"Yeah. I'm building a bookshelf for Meghan for her birthday."

"That couldn't have taken more than a few hours."

"I had some other projects I was working on too."

"Were you alone?"

Clint gave him a sideways glance. "Why? Are you my pastor now too?"

He didn't care for the bite in his brother's tone, but he let it go. Clint had had a lot of trouble in his life, and Bryce bore some of the responsibility for it. "No, I was only curious if you had anyone with you. Anyone who can attest you were where you said you were."

Clint picked up his coffee cup to take a sip then set it down, his face ashen. "Why are you asking me about an alibi, Bryce?"

"Another woman was abducted the night before last, Clint. She managed to escape and I found her."

He gulped hard. "Did she see who grabbed her?"

Bryce shook his head and watched his brother for signs. He was hoping he didn't see relief on his face. Clint's expression was bland, but he did seem worried.

He stood up. "I—I've been here alone. I don't have an alibi, Bryce. They're going to say I did this, aren't they?"

He knew as well as Clint that the police would zero in on him.

"There's something else," Bryce told him. "The woman, Lucy, she's an FBI profiler who's in town to help find the person who's been abducting these women. She said she scratched the man on the arm while she was fighting with him. They took skin samples from beneath her fingernails."

He scratched at the bandage on his arm and glared at his brother. "And now you see this and wonder if I did it, don't you? I didn't."

"I want to believe you, Clint, but that bandage…it's

throwing me for a loop. It's right where she said she scratched the guy."

He rolled up his sleeve and pulled off the bandage, revealing several stitches. "I cut myself with the saw. I nearly passed out from the pain, but I managed to get to the ER to have it stitched up." He rebandaged his arm. "I'm sure they're calling the police as we speak."

He had some hope. Clint's wound didn't look like he'd been scratched. It looked like what he said it was, a cut from a table saw. "Why didn't you call me? I would have driven you to the hospital."

Clint shrugged. "Like I told you, I'm used to doing things on my own when you're out of the country."

He heard a car outside and walked to the window. Apparently, Clint's guess had been correct. Two police cruisers were pulling into the lot. "Looks like you were right. They did call the police. They're here now."

Clint sighed and leaned against a chair. "When will this nightmare be over?"

Bryce opened the door and stepped out as two officers he knew got out of the car. "What can I do for you, Josh?" Josh Whitley was an acquaintance from church, while he'd met the other guy, Leonard Stubblefield, when Clint had been arrested for a previous DUI.

Josh did the talking. "We're here to take Clint in for questioning. Please send him out. We'll be impounding his car too in order to search it. The wrecker is on its way."

Clint stood behind him but stepped outside. "I'm here," he said. "No reason to cause a fuss."

Stubblefield handcuffed him, then led him away.

Bryce watched, knowing there was nothing he could

do to help his baby brother. He felt helpless and uncertain. But he knew one thing for sure.

His brother was being railroaded, and Lucy Sanderson was their only hope of proving his innocence.

Lucy hung around the police precinct and typed up a list of questions for the detectives to utilize during questioning. Detective Ross was at first skeptical of using them until Lucy reminded him that previous interviews between his detectives and the suspect had resulted in no new leads. He reluctantly agreed to examine her questions and pass them along to his detectives.

She watched through the interrogation room's window as Clint Tippitt was brought in and seated. Although she noticed a slight resemblance to Bryce, no hint of recognition flashed through her when she saw him. Nothing about him brought back memories of the man who had abducted her from the roadside. But her ability to identify her attacker was obviously limited. He could be standing in front of her, and she might not even know it.

She didn't stay for the questioning. She was already weary and ready to get back to the B&B and rest. And the detectives conducting the questioning seemed to be taking the same approach with Clint as they had in the past—accusations and demands for answers. And he had entered the room already on the defense. She doubted this interview would yield any new information.

In the lobby she spotted Bryce sitting in the waiting area chairs. His shoulders were slumped, and he looked defeated. She wished there was something she could do to comfort him.

"I guess you heard?" he asked as she took the seat beside him.

"I did. Were you with him when he was arrested?"

"Yes. He was at his workshop, as I'd suspected. Alone. There's no one who can verify his whereabouts for the past two days."

She leaned back into the chair beside him, knowing his worst fears were coming true.

"I know I promised to stay by your side," he began, but Lucy shushed him.

"You need to be with your brother. I completely understand."

"I feel like I'm letting you down too."

She reached out, took his hand and held it. "You're not letting anyone down, Bryce. You're doing everything you can to help the people you care about."

"I know I can't do anything sitting here, but I feel like I need to stay. If they don't find anything they can charge him with, he'll need a ride home. If they do…"

Lucy stood and leaned into him, pulling him into a hug. He seemed to need it, and she was glad to offer one. "Where's Meghan?"

"I texted her grandmother to pick her up from school today. She can stay with them for a day or two."

"I'll take a cab back to the B&B."

He rubbed her shoulders. "I should take you."

"No, you stay with your brother. I'll be fine. Let me know if anything changes."

She stayed with him until her cab arrived, then Bryce walked her to it and they said goodbye.

Once at the B&B, Lucy kicked off her heels and slid into a soft chair in Mrs. Ferguson's living room before catching her up on the day's events, including Clint's arrest.

"Bryce is beating himself up over this," Lucy confided. "I want to help him, but I don't know how."

Mrs. Ferguson only nodded. "Bryce is a good man. He takes on the burdens of others. His father was that way too."

Lucy was surprised to hear Mrs. Ferguson mention Bryce's father. "You knew him?"

"Of course. Everyone did. He was very popular around town. A very friendly man, charming and well-liked. Similar to Bryce."

"Then you must have been surprised when he was accused of killing a woman." It felt wrong to grill Mrs. Ferguson about Bryce's past, but now that he'd opened up to Lucy about his father, she longed to know more. While it might not have a connection to the cases she was working, it had an impact on Bryce, and she realized she was growing to care about him despite her determination not to.

"Oh yes, yes," Mrs. Ferguson continued. "We all were shocked. The affair wasn't such a surprise—it is a small town, you know—but the murder. That poor woman. I would have never believed John Tippitt was capable of that. Of course, these murders happening now, well, I've never seen such evil in my life. It seems this world continues to decline. If I didn't have my faith to fall back on, I don't know how I would survive it all."

Lucy wasn't surprised to learn Mrs. Ferguson was a woman of faith. Her Bible sat next to the armchair where Lucy knew she spent her mornings before break-fast and her evenings before bed.

Faith had always been important to Lucy too...until Danny's death had revealed to her that everything she'd thought she'd known was a lie. After that, she'd been too angry to pray, too devastated to turn to God and too doubtful to trust in a heavenly father who had let her down.

"I should get busy," Mrs. Ferguson told her, standing up and straightening the apron she wore. "My church is having a bake sale, and I promised to make two of my coconut pies. They're always a hit."

She disappeared into the kitchen, leaving Lucy alone with her thoughts. They inevitably turned back to Bryce. She'd grown closer to him than she'd intended to and she wanted to ease his burdens, yet she still had no way of discounting his brother's involvement in Jessica Nelson's disappearance and no way of preventing the local police from charging Clint for the deaths of the other women. While she doubted the case they had against Clint would ever be enough to convict him in a court of law, the process of being arrested and charged was stressful enough. The only way she could help was to find a lead to the real killer.

Lucy closed her eyes, intending to rest for only a few minutes before digging back into the case files, but the gentle hum from Mrs. Ferguson working in the kitchen and lack of sleep from the two previous nights finally caught up to her. When she opened her eyes again, she was surprised to find she had napped for two hours.

She regretted the lost time, but had to admit she felt better. Her mind was sharper and the ache in her head had lessened to a dull throbbing pain. She got up and went into the kitchen, poured herself a glass of water, then swallowed two Tylenol pills.

"Bryce hasn't phoned, has he?" She hated being without her cell phone, and wanted to replace it as soon as possible.

"He hasn't, dear, but someone left you a package at the door. I placed it on the dining room table."

Lucy glanced at the table and saw another box similar to the ones she'd received from the police. The side label stated it was additional case files. She was about to chide Mrs. Ferguson for lifting the heavy box, but then she slid it toward her and realized it wasn't heavy at all. It couldn't contain many files. And if there had been additional files she needed, why hadn't they given them to her while she was at the precinct earlier?

She lifted the top from the box and heard a click. Odd. She glanced inside, and instead of case files, she saw a small device with a timer and what looked like explosives wrapped in tape.

All the oxygen seemed to leave her lungs as she realized she'd just triggered a bomb when she'd lifted the top. The timer showed one minute and quickly started counting down the seconds.

Lucy dropped it and screamed for Mrs. Ferguson to get out of the house. She turned and ran into the kitchen, urging the woman to run out the back door.

Neither of them made it out before the explosion sent them both flying. Lucy was slammed against the refrigerator, then hit the floor. Her ears were ringing, and her whole body felt as if it was vibrating from the blast. She coughed, choking on the dust that settled around her.

She opened her eyes and looked around at the damage. Mrs. Ferguson was a few feet away, sprawled on the floor, unmoving. Lucy wanted to rush to her side to check on her, but she couldn't. Her body wouldn't move and she realized she was trapped, the refrigerator pinning her down.

A noise from behind her reached her ears, and she managed to turn her head to see flames shooting into the doorway from the dining room. It was fully engulfed and the fire was spreading quickly.

If help didn't arrive soon, they were both going to die.

FOUR

Bryce noticed the commotion at the precinct and heard sirens blare as several police cars rushed from the station parking lot.

He spotted Jim Ross heading out and stopped him. "What's going on? Has something happened?"

"I'm afraid so. We received a call about a fire at the Ferguson B&B. Fire and ambulance are already on the way. I'm heading there now too."

Lucy.

He never should have let her go alone.

"I'm going too."

He hitched a ride with Ross, knowing it would get him to the scene faster. By the time they turned onto the street, he saw flames shooting up from the ceiling and his heart clenched. He jumped from the police car and scanned the scene for Lucy, fear pressing into him as he realized she wasn't there.

He rushed to the fire chief, who was shouting commands and overseeing the hooking up of the hoses. "Is anyone still inside?" Bryce asked him.

"We don't know yet."

Bryce noticed the flames through the front windows in the dining room and knew the front door would be inaccessible, but perhaps he could still get into the house through the back door. He ran toward the side of the house, the chief calling for him to get back.

He rounded the corner and saw the back door standing open. Black smoke flowed through it, and when he glanced inside, he couldn't see anything. The smoke was too thick. But he thought he heard something. He stood at the door for a moment and listened, hearing it again ever so faintly. A voice calling out for help.

"Here!" Bryce called. "I hear someone inside."

He didn't wait for help though. He rushed inside and pressed through the smoke, calling out for Lucy and Mrs. Ferguson. The roar of the fire in the next room was loud, and he spotted flames crawling up the curtains. It would spread here very soon and possibly block his getting back out, but he couldn't leave without at least searching.

His foot hit on something, and he knelt and felt a figure. Mrs. Ferguson. She was unconscious but alive. Two firefighters in full gear entered the house, and he called to them. One slung Mrs. Ferguson over his shoulder and carried her out.

"You need to get out of here too," he said, trying to pull Bryce out, but he refused.

"Not yet. I have to find Lucy."

The other firefighter used his flashlight to scan the area, and Bryce spotted movement in the corner near the overturned refrigerator. "There!" he said, and together they rushed over and found Lucy.

She glanced up at him, her face covered in soot and her green eyes bright with tears. But she was alive!

Together, Bryce and the firefighter heaved the refrigerator off her and freed her legs, but when she tried to stand, she couldn't. Bryce swept her up into his arms and hurried out the back door.

He raced her toward the waiting ambulance and placed her on the gurney. Two paramedics hurried to help, one attending to Lucy and the other to him, offering him oxygen. He started to wave away the paramedic's help, but stopped when he sat down and realized he was having a hard time breathing. He shouldn't have rushed in. He'd ignored the chief's orders not to go inside, but it wasn't the first time he'd ignored orders.

He'd found Lucy, and that was all that mattered.

Sweet oxygen.

Her throat burned as the paramedic placed the plastic mask over her face and she breathed in fresh air.

She saw Bryce sit down and noticed the toll coming in for her had taken on him. She was grateful, but she was also concerned about Mrs. Ferguson and finding out who'd done this.

Chief Dobson soon approached her. He wanted answers, and so did she.

"How is Mrs. Ferguson?" Lucy demanded. Her throat hurt, and her voice sounded weak and strained from smoke inhalation.

"She's fine," he assured her. "She has a gash on her head that will probably need stiches and she's suffered some smoke inhalation, but she'll be fine. Is anyone else inside the house?"

Lucy shook her head. "I was trying to get Mrs. Ferguson out the back door when the bomb exploded."

He looked stunned and so did Bryce, who turned and gaped at her.

"Bomb?" Bryce asked. "What bomb?"

"Someone delivered a box to the house addressed to me. When I opened it, I triggered the detonator." Whoever was behind these attacks had taken pity on Mrs. Ferguson previously, but not this time. Apparently, he was no longer concerned about sparing her.

Lucy stared past their shocked expressions to the house still in flames. "Can they save it?"

Chief Dobson shook his head. "The fire chief doesn't think so. It'll be a total loss."

Lucy closed her eyes and let that sink in. Mrs. Ferguson had lost everything, all her belongings and even her home, all in someone's effort to kill Lucy. When Lucy captured the person responsible, she would make them pay. That was a promise she would make for what he'd done to her, but also the collateral damage he'd heaped on Mrs. Ferguson.

"I'd like to see Mrs. Ferguson," Lucy stated.

"You will soon enough. They're taking you to the hospital for evaluation." She was about to protest that she didn't need to go when Chief Dobson held out his hand. "Don't even argue. You're going. I don't need this to be a fatality after all. Smoke can do serious damage to your lungs. Go and get yourself checked out. There's nothing you can do here. Once they finish dousing the fire, the fire marshal will determine how it started and examine whatever is left of the device." He glanced at

Bryce. "You go too. We'll talk later about your reck-lessness at running inside."

Bryce stepped into the ambulance and sat down, and only then did Lucy fully realize how he'd risked his life to rush in to find her. Chief Dobson was right that it had been reckless, but she was grateful anyway. She'd thought she would die inside that house tonight, but her attacker had failed to kill her once again.

Hopefully, once they examined the bomb, they could determine where it had come from, and some forensic evidence would point the way to the person targeting her.

He'd come too close to winning tonight.

Bryce settled onto a hospital bed in the emergency room and allowed the doctor to examine him, but he balked at the idea of being kept overnight for observa-tion. He needed to get to Lucy to make certain she was okay after her ordeal, and he needed to phone Meghan to let her know he was okay before she heard about the fire and his involvement from someone else. Plus his brother was still sitting in a jail cell.

Cassidy came into the room and stared at him, her folded arms a sign of disapproval. "What were you thinking running into that house?" she asked as she settled an oxygen mask over his face.

She was his closest friend and had been for as long as he could remember, but he couldn't tell her the truth—that he hadn't been thinking of anything except find-ing Lucy no matter the cost. Yes, it had been dumb, but he'd acted on instinct and fallen back on his training to run into danger when others ran out.

Cassidy continued to fuss at him. "What if you'd been killed? What would happen to Meghan?"

It wasn't something he liked to think about, but he'd had to face it given the dangers of his job as a covert operative. It helped him to know Meghan still had her grandparents if something happened to him.

"I'm fine," he assured Cassidy, pulling off the mask to speak.

She sighed and fell into a chair beside him. "You're taking too many risks for this woman, Bryce. You hardly even know her."

Although that was true, he felt like he'd known Lucy for years, and he'd already witnessed her selflessness and kind nature firsthand. And without her help, Bryce was sure his brother would soon be in prison labeled forever as a serial killer.

"I need her," he told Cassidy, hoping she couldn't see his desire for Lucy had gone past the professional point. He was falling for her hard, and in such a short time.

Cassidy pulled the oxygen mask back over his face. "What you need is rest." She walked out and left him alone.

She wasn't wrong. He had taken an unnecessary risk rushing into that house. But as he thought about seeing Lucy lying on the floor, he knew he would do it again in a heartbeat.

Spending another night at the hospital hadn't been in her plans, but since the B&B had burned down, she wasn't resisting the doctor's recommendation to stay the night for observation. However, sleep wasn't going to come for Lucy until she knew Mrs. Ferguson was all right. She convinced a nurse to wheel her into the older woman's hospital room.

Mrs. Ferguson was lying in the hospital bed when she entered, but reached out for Lucy when she saw her. "I'm so glad to see you. I was so worried about you."

"I'm fine," Lucy assured her. "How are you?"

"Fine, fine. Just some scrapes and smoke inhalation." Her expression darkened. "Chief Dobson and the fire marshal were here a little while ago. They managed to put out the blaze, but there was so much damage to the house that they don't know if it can be saved or if I'll have to rebuild."

Lucy felt the blow of that statement. Mrs. Ferguson had lost her home because of her, because someone had placed a target on her back. "I'm so sorry," Lucy told her. "What will you do now?"

"I've already spoken to my sister. I'll go and stay with her for a while." She grabbed Lucy's hand. "What will you do, dear?" She'd lost everything tonight, yet she was still worried about others.

"I'll be fine," Lucy assured her. And she would not allow this maniac to hurt anyone else in her name.

Now that she'd seen Mrs. Ferguson, exhaustion pulled at her and she knew she would rest, but when she returned to her room and found Bryce waiting for her, rest was the last thing on her mind. He pulled her into a hug, and she soaked in the feel of him. She wanted to melt into his arms and finally release the fear and anguish of nearly being killed. Again.

"How are you?" he asked as he stroked her hair tenderly.

"I'm fine. I got away with only minor burns and

some smoke inhalation." She touched his face and felt the stubble on his cheek. Soot still outlined his face and arms, but they only served to remind her that this man had risked his life for her.

"I'm getting tired of this guy targeting you."

"Me too."

"Doesn't he know that killing an FBI agent will surely bring other FBI agents into town to hunt him down?"

"That's true, but I don't think this perpetrator is thinking that logically. He wants me out of the way, and he's willing to go to great lengths to make it happen. This feels personal."

She shuddered at her own realization. Somehow, in the past two days, she'd done something to anger someone so much that they'd resorted to attempted murder. And whoever was behind this had already accelerated from protecting Mrs. Ferguson to not caring if she was hurt or not. Yet she couldn't think of anyone who might have such hostility toward her, or anything she'd done to anger someone to that degree.

That brought her back full circle to the serial killer who'd abducted her. This had all started with him, and although the attacks against her once she'd escaped him didn't match his modus operandi, she had to believe she was under attack because of her involvement in this case. Someone wanted her to stop investigating and leave town.

But who? And why?

"I think someone wants me to stop looking for this serial killer."

"But you're not going to, are you." It wasn't a question as much as a comment, and she smiled. He already knew her so well.

"Absolutely not." She'd come to town to catch a bad guy. Might as well catch two while she was at it.

After being released from the hospital the next day, Lucy checked into a local hotel, but she didn't plan on spending much time there.

Bryce picked her up from the hotel and drove her into town to do some shopping. He was feeling better, having recovered from the smoke inhalation. Plus he'd learned his brother was a free man once again. As she'd suspected, the interrogating officers hadn't gotten any of the answers they'd sought, and after several hours of questioning Clint, had been forced to release him.

All of her clothes and accessories had been casualties of the fire, so she needed to replace some items until she knew what could be salvaged. Even her service weapon had been damaged. After purchasing a couple of new outfits and some toiletries and picking up a cell phone, she and Bryce stopped for lunch at a diner in town.

"Do you want to get sandwiches to go and take them back to the precinct?" he asked, and she agreed that was a good idea.

She wanted to spend the afternoon focusing her attention back on the serial killer. That had to be her priority, at least until the police finished processing the evidence from the bombing to see if it led to a particular person. Detective Ross had arranged for her to set up and work out of one of the conference rooms at the police precinct. She thought that was better, in case of another attack against her. She didn't want any evidence that might be in her possession to be destroyed.

She sat in Bryce's truck while he went inside to pick up their food. While waiting, she heard a squeal and saw Meghan jump from a car that had pulled into the parking lot and hurry over to the truck's window.

A woman closer to Lucy's age parked then followed, her eyes narrowing at Lucy. She looked familiar but Lucy couldn't place her at first—then she recalled having seen her at the hospital. Bryce's nurse friend.

"I'm so glad to see you. Are you okay?" Meghan opened the door and pulled her into a hug.

"I'm okay, Meghan. Just some scratches and soreness."

"I was so worried about you," Meghan said. "When I heard what had happened, I burst into tears. I'm so thankful you and my dad are okay. And poor Mrs. Ferguson too. Cassidy and I just came from the hospital visiting her. We brought her a card and some flowers. She told us she's leaving town to stay with her sister."

"Yes, she told me that too. I was sorry to hear it."

Meghan groaned. "I'm sorry. I forgot to introduce you. Cassidy, this is Lucy. She's with the FBI. How cool is that? Lucy, this is Cassidy Summers."

Lucy shook the other woman's hand. "I recognize you from the hospital. You're Bryce's friend, right?"

"That's right. Bryce and I have been friends forever."

Lucy didn't miss the possessive bite in her tone when she said the word *forever*. Was something going on between Cassidy and Bryce that she wasn't aware of? He hadn't told her he was seeing someone, but her face burned with shame as she realized she didn't know, yet she'd still fallen into his arms last night. "It's nice to meet you, Cassidy."

"Same here. You and Bryce seem to have been spending quite a lot of time together over the past few days."

Lucy was glad Meghan didn't seem to pick up on the tension Cassidy was sending out. "Things have been crazy since I came to town. I'm thankful he's been there to help me."

"I'll say it's been crazy. Like everyone else in town, I was shocked to hear about an explosion at the B&B. It's tragic," Cassidy said. "Why would anyone want to hurt that old woman?"

Again, Lucy felt her face flush with shame. "I believe Mrs. Ferguson was collateral damage. I was the one they were after."

Bryce arrived at the truck with their food and two drinks stuffed into a plastic tray. He grinned when he spotted his daughter and Cassidy.

"What are you two doing here?" he asked, giving Meghan a kiss on the head. She couldn't help noticing he didn't have one for Cassidy.

"We just came from visiting with Mrs. Ferguson," Cassidy said. "Now I'm taking Meghan back to her grandmother's house. I have a shift at the hospital in a few hours." She turned back to Lucy. "Bryce tells me he brought you to town to find the Back Roads Killer and clear his brother's name. How's that going?" Her tone again seemed clearly hostile to Lucy, but both Bryce and Meghan seemed unfazed. Was it possible she was imagining things?

"Well, the police don't seem to have any physical

evidence tying Clint to those crimes, but I can see they want to pin them on him. Hopefully, I can identify another suspect for them to investigate."

"My uncle Clint is innocent," Meghan said. She grabbed Lucy's hands. "You have to prove to them that he didn't do it. You have to."

"I hope your investigation goes well," Cassidy said before leading Meghan off.

"I'll do my best," Lucy called to Meghan, although lately, her best wasn't what it should have been. She'd once been a respectable profiler and considered herself good at her job. She'd helped identify numerous killers and aided departments in bringing safety back to their communities…but that had been before Danny, before she'd discovered how blind she could be and her confidence had taken a nosedive. Now, she couldn't help wondering if her profiling skills were even that good. After all, if she couldn't even see what her own fiancé had been doing right under her nose, how could she ever expect to understand the inner workings of a killer's mind?

All she could do now was fall back on her training and hope for the best.

When they arrived at the police station, Detective Ross approached them as they entered the precinct. "I set you up in the back conference room on the left. No one will bother you in there. I had copies of all the task force case files placed there as well as the new evidence we collected at your abduction site." He leaned in to whisper to her as he slipped her a file out of Bryce's eyesight. "This is the file on Bryce's father's case that you asked for."

She quietly thanked him then slipped the file into her new shoulder bag. "Any news on the bomb fragments?" she asked, bringing Bryce back into the conversation.

He shook his head. "Not officially. The fire marshal is still examining the scene, but he believes it was a homemade bomb containing fertilizer and other easily obtained items. If that's the case, anyone could be responsible. We finished canvassing the neighborhood, but no one saw the person who delivered it."

"It had to be someone who knew I was there. Most arsonists like to stick around to watch the fire blaze. Bombers are no different. Can you get me a list of the people who were there?"

"No problem. We might even have video of the crowd. I noticed someone recorded the scene on their cell phone and posted it online this morning. I'll pull it up and we'll take a look."

Ross grabbed his computer and met them in the conference room. He opened the social media page and clicked on the video of the B&B blaze. Lucy noticed it was posted on a page that belonged to someone named James McIntyre.

"Do you know this guy who made the recording?" she asked, and both Bryce and Ross affirmed they did.

"He's a high school kid," Bryce said. "He works as a cashier at the gas station around the corner from Mrs. Ferguson's B&B."

"I attend church with his family," Ross said. "He's a good kid. I can't see him involved in any of this."

She also doubted he was involved since he'd posted

the recording online, but they would still have to question him to be certain. She watched the screen closely, trying not to think about the blaze that had nearly killed her and destroyed a dear older woman's belongings. Instead, she tried to concentrate on the crowd as the recorder moved his camera around the area.

"I see a lot of familiar faces," Bryce said.

"Me too," Ross agreed. "Hard for me to believe any of them are involved."

She understood it was hard for them to imagine that one of their neighbors, perhaps even someone they'd known for years, could be involved, but they had to consider it. "Do you notice anyone acting suspicious or out of character?" She didn't personally see anyone that made her radar perk up, but Bryce and Ross knew these people and might notice something out of the ordinary.

She restarted the video, but neither man noticed anything suspicious.

She sighed and closed the computer, happy to not have to look at those images again. "Bombers usually like to see the destruction their act causes. The fact that he wasn't there watching reinforces my belief that, to the person who did this, the bomb was merely a tool for them to get what they want. He'll use whatever means possible to achieve his mission."

"You dead," Bryce said.

"He wants me dead for some personal reason I can't fathom. There's no inciting event I can place my finger on. The only thing I did after coming to town before these threats and attacks started was get abducted by the serial killer."

"And you still don't believe this has anything to do with the Back Roads Killer?" Ross asked her.

Even though the attacker had upped his game, the behavior still didn't match what she knew about the killer. She still believed she was dealing with two very different people.

"I don't, but we might be dealing with someone who doesn't want this killer found. Perhaps he's acting on the killer's behalf. A friend? A family member? Someone who knows his secret and will go to any lengths to keep him from being discovered?"

"Who would do something like that?" Bryce asked. "I mean, I would do almost anything for my brother, but if I thought he was guilty, I couldn't cover it up, especially through even more violence."

"Not everyone shares your moral compass," Lucy reminded him. "Unless the fire marshal finds something that can point us toward the bomber, we're at a dead end."

"I'll start checking on the list of ingredients used to make the bomb," Ross told her. "Maybe I can find out where they were purchased and who bought them."

She nodded and handed him back his computer. "I appreciate that. I'm going to turn my attention back to the Back Roads Killer case."

If they didn't identify this man soon, no one in town—or around her, anyway—was safe.

Lucy opened the box that contained the evidence collected at the scene on the side of the road where she'd been abducted. Inside the box, she found several bagged items, including her old cell phone, headphones and identification. She also found notations of tire marks and blood on the gravel.

She shuddered, recalling the terror she'd felt in that moment. This had always been a job to her. In her line of work, you had to try to disconnect, or the terrible things you saw would drive you insane. But she couldn't disconnect this time. This had happened to her. She stared at the wall of photos of the other victims' bodies. She might have been one of them if not for different circumstances. If the killer had been able to inject her with that needle, she would be on this wall now.

She shuddered, and Bryce stared at her in concern. "You okay?"

"I could have ended up there. Victim number four."

He put his arms around her and pulled her to him. "But you didn't. You used your brains and your training to escape him."

"No, I was captured. It was only luck that kept him from injecting me. If he had, I wouldn't be here today."

He shook his head. "Not luck. God's intervention."

She pulled away from him. "But why? I don't deserve any special treatment. I'm certainly no better than these other women. Why did I deserve God's intervention? In fact, I'm probably worse. I should be dead."

"Don't say that, Lucy."

"It's true. You have no idea the things I've done, Bryce. You don't even know me."

"Then introduce me." He tucked a strand of hair behind her ear, then locked eyes with her. "I'd like to get to know you better."

She wanted that too, but she was afraid of going down that road. He might not like what he discovered.

Then she recalled the possessive vibe she'd gotten from Cassidy earlier. "Is something going on with you and Cassidy? Are you two an item?"

"No, we're friends. That's all. Do you think I'd be here with you if there was someone else in my life?"

"I'd hope not." He was either blind to Cassidy's feelings for him, or she was the one misreading everything. "I can't deny I'm incredibly drawn to you, Bryce, but this is all happening so fast in such a short time."

"It is happening fast, and I understand if you need to back off, but Lucy, don't do it because you think there's something about you I can't handle. We all have things in our pasts we regret. It doesn't make us less deserving of God's love."

She looked away as the guilt of the Williams family washed over her. "You can't say that. You don't know."

He touched her face, his fingers stroking her lips. She wanted to fall into his arms and dig her head into his shoulder, but if he knew what she'd done, he would surely turn and run.

"I've done terrible things myself, Lucy. Making mistakes isn't exclusive to you."

"Have you killed people?" The image of the crash scene filled her mind, the twisted metal and the bodies of an innocent family. She glanced up at him and swallowed hard. She hadn't meant to say that, but he was staring at her for several long seconds, during which she thought he would probably leave.

Instead, his eyes darkened and he nodded. "I have."

She saw pain behind his answer. He had his own wounds. Of course he did. But he'd been a soldier. It had been his job to make those tough choices. "You did your job," she said.

He nodded. "I did my job. And I would do it again if it meant saving the lives of innocent people."

She turned away as tears pressed at her eyes. "What—what if those people you killed were the innocents?" The thought of those children Danny had killed continued to plague her. If only she'd seen what he was doing. If only she'd stopped him.

She felt him behind her. "Lucy, tell me what happened."

"I—I can't talk about it." She pulled herself together and quickly gathered her papers. He might be okay with learning she'd shot a suspect threatening someone's life, but it would be a different story if he knew she'd been party to killing an innocent family in a minivan.

"Please take me back to the hotel." She saw his hesitation. He wanted to push her for answers. She jutted her chin and pushed back the tears. "Please, Bryce, take me back to the hotel."

Finally he nodded, and she hurried outside. She didn't even wait for him to open the door for her, despite how much she liked that particular tendency of his. It just proved to her what a good man he really was. He deserved someone equally good. She didn't qualify. She could never be the person good enough for Bryce.

He climbed into the truck and tried to make small talk as he drove, but she couldn't respond. If she started talking, she knew she would fall apart. She wanted to get back to her room and let her tears fall, along with her anger at Danny. He'd done this to her. He'd put her in this position. She wanted to hate him, but she couldn't.

She jumped from the cab of the truck when he parked at the hotel, but he was right behind her. "I'll walk you upstairs."

She wanted to protest but knew it wouldn't do any good. He was walking her to her room whether she liked it or not.

They rode the elevator to the fourth floor, and Bryce walked her to the door.

He stopped her before she put in her key card and forced her to look at him. "I don't know what is going on inside that head of yours, Lucy, but I want you to know there is nothing you could tell me that would change the way I feel about you."

She wanted to believe that. He was a good and loyal man. She'd seen it up close and personal, yet she also knew if he discovered his brother was responsible for these deaths, he wouldn't hesitate to turn him in to the police to face justice. He wouldn't understand her inability to see the truth about Danny. How could he? She didn't even understand it herself.

He touched her face and gently placed a kiss on her forehead. His hand slid down her arm, and she felt the skin prickle at his touch. How she wanted to lean into him! Yet she fought her own instincts. She had to.

His hand found hers, and he took the key card from her. "Let me check the room before you go inside."

She felt heat rush up her neck. Here she'd been thinking he was getting friendly, but he was really looking after her safety. She hadn't even been thinking about checking the room. That was how out of sorts she was, and how deeply this burgeoning relationship was affecting her. She had to put a stop to it.

He stuck the card into the lock and it clicked. Bryce pulled his gun from his holster and pushed open the door, flicking on the light. Lucy stepped in behind him and held open the door. The room appeared empty, but Bryce wasn't taking any chances. She liked that about him. He was thorough and assured. He checked the closet and behind the curtains. The room was empty, and nothing appeared to have been moved.

He opened the bathroom door, and when he did, a blast of gunfire sent Lucy stumbling backward in shock and surprise into the hallway. Her ears were ringing and she was momentarily stunned, but the realization that a gun had gone off had her scrambling back to her feet and into the room.

The blast had thrown Bryce backward too, onto the edge of the bed. He was holding his shoulder and blood was pooling between his fingers. He slipped off the bed and to the floor as Lucy rushed to him. Pain riddled his face, and he'd grown pale.

But before she could tend to him, she had to take care of the shooter. She picked up Bryce's gun from the floor and kicked open the bathroom door, ready to confront the shooter, but all she saw was a rifle hanging from a wire attached to the ceiling. There was no shooter, only an elaborate booby trap rigged to fire whenever she opened the door.

She rushed back to Bryce. "I—I think I'm okay," he told her, but she could see he wasn't.

"I'm calling for an ambulance."

"I'm not leaving you," he barked. "Someone set a booby trap in your room. That was meant for you, Lucy.

It hit me in the shoulder, but it would have been a head shot for you."

She glanced at his shoulder and realized he was right.

Whoever had set this trap had intended to kill her, but Bryce had opened the door first. He'd taken the bullet that was meant for her.

FIVE

The gunshot proved to be a through and through. It hadn't done any damage but it sure did hurt, especially when Bryce moved his arm. He groaned in pain and Cassidy, who'd been on duty when the ambulance brought him in and had taken over his care, shot him an I-told-you-so look.

"That woman nearly got you killed, Bryce," she said as she bandaged his wound. "Again!"

"It wasn't her fault, Cassidy. I was clearing the room and someone had set a trap."

"I don't understand why she's still here. If someone tried to kill me several times, I would have left town by now."

"She's determined and brave. It's one of the things I like about her."

Cassidy cut off a piece of bandage and looked at him before applying it. "Are you falling for this woman, Bryce?"

Her question caught him off guard because he hadn't realized how obvious his growing feelings for Lucy were. He couldn't deny them. He liked her more and more each day, and the desire to protect her grew with it. It had been a long time since he'd given a relationship a real chance, not since the fiasco with Meghan's mother had left him cynical about women and relationships. He couldn't say he was ready to jump into one again, but the more time he spent with Lucy, the more he was considering taking that risk someday.

The door to his hospital room opened and Meghan rushed inside, followed by Lucy.

"She was outside in the hall," Lucy said as Meghan fell into his arms. He grimaced as she jarred his shoulder, but he wrapped his uninjured arm around her.

"Hey, I'm okay," he assured her. "It was just a bullet to the shoulder. I'm fine. I don't even need surgery. Tell her, Cassidy."

"It's true. His shoulder is fine. It's his head that needs to be examined, in my opinion." She shot Lucy a glance, then finished bandaging him.

"You have to be more careful," Meghan said, tears streaming down her face. "I can't lose you too."

Those words stabbed at his heart. His daughter was right. He needed to be more careful for her sake. He pulled her tighter against him and reassured her again that he was okay. He was used to danger in his life as a covert operative, but that was thousands of miles away in another country, and his daughter had never had to witness it. The last two times he'd been shot had been before Meghan had come into his life, so seeing him this way had to shake her. But as he glanced over her head to Lucy, he grew conflicted. He'd brought her here and placed her life in danger all in the interest of clearing Clint's name. He couldn't abandon her now.

Cassidy had asked him why Lucy didn't leave town, and although he didn't have an exact answer since he'd never asked her that question, he recognized something of himself in her. She wasn't going to leave while a monster was still attacking women, and she wasn't going to allow someone to target her without finding out who it was and why.

It wasn't in her DNA. She had spunk, and he found that a super attractive trait.

But his two highest priorities were in direct conflict with one another.

Lucy stepped out of Bryce's hospital room and leaned against the wall as emotion threatened to overtake her. Tears slid down her cheeks. He'd been hurt because of her, just as Mrs. Ferguson had been injured and lost everything. Meghan's cries to her father had only reinforced what Lucy knew. She couldn't continue to risk people's lives this way. She was a one-woman wrecking ball.

She pulled herself together and walked back into the room to find Bryce sitting up on the bed and Meghan helping him pull on his jacket. "What do you think you're doing?" Lucy demanded.

"I've already talked to the police and I've had my wound bandaged. Now, I want to go home," he told her. "I'm not staying here."

"I don't think you've been cleared by the doctors."

His eyes pleaded with her. "I can't stay here. The doctor gave me painkillers. There's nothing else they can do for me here that I can't do at home."

Cassidy looked as put out with Bryce as Lucy felt,

but even she could tell she wasn't going to change his mind. "If you insist on this foolishness, make sure you keep the bandage clean and change it periodically. Don't get it wet, and if you see any indications of infection, call us or come back in. Infection is the biggest danger to him right now."

"Don't worry," Meghan told her. "We'll take care of him."

Once he'd been discharged, Lucy pulled the truck around and Meghan helped him climb into the passenger's seat. He grimaced with pain, and Lucy felt a vindictive pleasure at seeing it. "You should have stayed at the hospital," she told him.

He shot her a glance at her unsympathetic tone. "You're not a nurturing type, are you?"

She ignored his jab and drove. Once home, Bryce fell into a recliner and sighed. "I already feel better. It's good to be home."

Meghan scrambled to get him what he needed. Lucy suspected the girl had to care for him in order to process his injury and near-death. "I'll fix you some supper. How does stew sound?"

He nodded. "It sounds terrific, Megs."

She hurried into the kitchen to start supper, and Bryce reached for Lucy. "Thank you for being here. Meghan is understandably upset."

"Of course she is. She's already lost her mother. Now her father has been shot."

"Lucy, I want you to stay here tonight."

Her eyes widened in shock. How could he ask that of her after what he'd been through? "I don't think that's a good idea."

"You can't go back to your hotel room. It's a crime scene."

"Then I'll get another room."

He gave her a small laugh. "After Mrs. Ferguson's and now this, I'm sure the people clamoring to rent you a room is a mile long."

She hadn't thought about that. Would she be able to get another place to stay? She supposed she could always find a cot at the police station.

Bryce took her hand. "Lucy, I'm in a lot of pain and about to take medicine that's going to knock me out for a while." He glanced toward the kitchen, and Lucy realized where his concern lay. "I need you to be here to protect Meghan. I can't let anything happen to her."

His request made more sense now. He was only looking out for his daughter's safety. "Of course I'll stay. I won't let anything happen to her, Bryce. That's a promise."

Less than an hour later, Bryce was asleep in the recliner, his gentle breathing a welcome relief from the pain she'd seen plastered on his face. Meghan had also fallen asleep on the couch beside his chair, refusing to leave her father's side in case he needed her. Lucy knew she was coping the only way she knew how, and she didn't press. They needed this time together.

But she wouldn't sleep tonight, not while Bryce had trusted her with his daughter's protection. Besides, she doubted sleep would come even if she wanted it to.

She settled into a chair at the kitchen table and took the case files from her shoulder bag. Detective Ross had slipped her the one on Bryce's father's supposed mistress, Amanda Lake, and she hadn't wanted to read it with him around. Now seemed like the perfect opportunity, when everyone was asleep and the house was quiet.

The report read like any of a hundred different cases she'd perused. A woman went missing, then was found dead two days later, her body dumped on the side of a back road. The police identified her as twenty-six-year-old Amanda Lake, a secretary at the Whitten Community Church. Officers questioned her friends and family, and discovered she'd been carrying on an affair with married man John Tippitt. He was questioned and confessed to the affair, but denied involvement in her death. Evidence was collected at the scene, but a DNA match was inconclusive.

The evidence against John appeared circumstantial, but Lucy understood why they looked at him as a prime suspect, just as she understood why Clint was suspected in his girlfriend's disappearance. Statistically, romantic partners were almost always involved when a woman went missing or was murdered.

Lucy pulled out the mug shot of John Tippitt and saw a remarkable resemblance to Bryce. He had the same dark blond hair and beard and blue eyes. In this photo, he would have been about the same age Bryce was now, yet he'd chosen to put his family at risk with his own selfishness then taken the easy way out when he'd been caught.

The photos of the victim were graphic. Her throat had been slashed, and she'd been posed in a manner that indicated the killer wanted to prove his control over her. It reminded Lucy a lot of the current murders, and she pulled up the images on her phone of the three victims. The scenes were similar enough to give her pause. The body had been dumped in a location like the ones where the three victims she'd attached to the Back Roads Killer had been found—a remote location close to a road where it would be discovered, and posed in the same way, to show the killer had control over the woman. The scene showed some signs of being sloppy, as more forensic evidence had been left behind for the police to find. But that could indicate this had been his first killing and that the killer had grown and learned through years of experience.

She glanced at Bryce sleeping peacefully. His father had committed suicide not long after the murder. That ruled him out as a suspect in the current cases, and if the cases were proven to be committed by the same offender, that ruled him out as Amanda Lake's killer, as well. And if Lake was truly the first victim, that made tying Jessica Nelson's disappearance to the case even more of a stretch.

Excitement filled her because first victims almost always had a personal connection to their killer, which meant her suspect pool had aged by twenty years. She closed the file and texted a message to Detective Ross to update her profile. The suspect had to be older, in his forties or fifties. She was officially listing Amanda Lake as the very first victim of the Back Roads Killer, tying her death to the other three victims, as well as Lucy's own attempted abduction.

She would have good news for Bryce when he awoke. She may have just ruled out his brother as a serial killer—and also exonerated his father.

"Is this true?" Bryce asked as he glanced through the case file of the woman his father had been accused of murdering. Lucy had told him her theory that Amanda Lake was the first victim of a killer who was still active.

"I believe it is." She stared at him, her eyes glowing with excitement at the possibility of making a real break in the case.

He was too stunned to speak, so he simply stood and pulled her into his embrace. She fit just right, and the sweet scent of her hair sent his mind spinning. She'd given him back his father—someone he'd thought he lost a long time ago.

His father was innocent.

His brother was innocent.

And maybe his family wasn't full of terrible monsters.

"What do we do now?"

"Well, I've messaged Detective Ross about getting the forensic evidence they collected from the Lake case to compare to DNA samples collected from the current crime scenes. If we can match it up, we can prove this is the same offender. The case file states they collected samples that didn't belong to Amanda Lake, so they assumed it belonged to the killer. It's not a guarantee, but it's a good place to start."

Finally, progress on the case. He'd waited so long for it and he owed this progress all to Lucy. Calling her in had been the best thing he could have done, and he was thankful God had pushed him in that direction. It was good to finally have someone on his side.

"We should also dig into Amanda Lake's life. It's likely she knew the person who killed her."

He wasn't sure he liked that idea. He'd spent years trying not to think about the woman he'd blamed for tearing apart their family. Now, Lucy wanted him to get to know her better. "I don't know much about her. I only vaguely remember her from when I was a kid."

"Does she still have family in town?"

"I don't think so. I don't know anything about her family."

Lucy opened the file and glanced through it. "According to the police notes, she wasn't from Whitten. She moved to town to take that job at the church as a secretary. Her only family was a sister from Atlanta. We should contact her."

"Would it help to talk to people who knew her at the time of her death?"

"Absolutely. Do you know any?"

"She worked at the church, and a lot of the longtime members knew her. Today is Sunday, and the service starts in an hour. We could go and ask around. I know Cassidy's parents will be there, and they certainly knew her. I'm sure there are others."

He watched her hesitate before agreeing, but he could see she wasn't thrilled with the idea of going to church. A moment ago she'd been excited to interview anyone who might have known Amanda Lake. Now, she looked edgy as she put away her files.

"Are you sure you're up for going out?" She motioned to his arm in a sling. "You're still recovering."

"After the news you gave me this morning, I feel great." It was true. His shoulder was sore, and he would deal with some pain and stiffness for a while, but he'd suffered worse injuries during his time as a marine and an SOA operator.

"I didn't bring a change of clothes with me last night.

I don't have anything to wear. Maybe we should do this another time."

"Today will be our best opportunity to talk to many people who were around when she was killed. I'm sure Meghan has something you can borrow to wear."

She didn't seem convinced, but she finally agreed. "I'll run upstairs and ask her." She rushed up the stairs.

Bryce wondered why she was so hesitant about going to church. Did it have anything to do with Danny and the way he'd died? She hadn't shared the details of his death yet, but Bryce could tell she was shouldering some of the blame. He didn't understand why. From what he'd read on the news site, she hadn't even been in the car when Danny had crashed into that van. Was it survivor's guilt? He knew a thing or two about that and how pervasive it could be.

Yet he could see she was trying so hard to keep her focus on the task at hand instead of dwelling on the past. He needed to do the same. His priority had to be catching this killer and keeping Lucy safe.

Maybe one day she would share her hurts with him.

What on earth was she doing in church?

She'd accepted Bryce's invitation to join him and Meghan because she wanted to have an opportunity to speak with several members who knew Bryce's parents as well as the woman who died. But as she sat in the pew, she felt she shouldn't be here. She had too much to atone for, and she hadn't even started.

She thought of the Williams family, who would never attend church again. They'd been deprived of worshipping together, of the kids learning about Jesus or joining youth group activities. She saw them in each family who entered and took a seat, and shame rolled through her like a tidal wave.

Bryce leaned close and put his arm around her. "You okay?"

She gripped her hands to keep them from shaking, but she couldn't stop the voices screaming in her soul that she didn't belong here. She shouldn't have come.

"I-I'm sorry. I shouldn't be here," she said, jumping from her seat and hurrying through the doors. Near the entryway, she fell into a chair and put her head in her hands.

A moment later the doors opened and Bryce slipped out. He knelt beside her. "Hey, what happened back there?"

She couldn't have stopped the tears even if she wanted to, but she shook her head. She couldn't speak. She didn't want him to know the terrible thing she'd done. Didn't want to see his face change into pity or repulsion at her inaction to stop the deaths of an entire family.

He didn't probe any further. Instead, he pulled a chair up beside her, held her hand and sat with her as she cried. His presence was a balm against the open wound of her heart, and even though she knew she shouldn't get so close to him, she couldn't pull away. She didn't want to. He would walk away from her soon enough, once he realized what a fraud she truly was. An FBI profiler who couldn't even see her own fiancé had a drug problem that caused the deaths of an entire family.

She felt sorry for Bryce and all he'd suffered. He didn't deserve such pain, and she didn't understand why he had to bear it. His shoulders were strong and she knew he could take a lot, but not this, not her shame. She would be humiliated when he uncovered it.

For now, she took comfort in his embrace and the calming presence of him. It was all she could ask for. He held her hand and leaned against her chair. From where they sat, she could hear what was happening in the sanctuary. Bryce hummed along with the music, and she recognized the song. "Amazing Grace." She'd learned it as a child and always loved it.

At some point during the hour, she realized she'd stopped crying. She'd been listening to the preacher's words and realized how much she missed this. Her faith used to be such a balm to her, but she hadn't had the nerve to step foot into a church since Danny's death.

As the service inside was coming to an end, she excused herself and hurried to the bathroom to clean herself up. Her eyes were red and puffy, and she felt like a fool for the display she'd put on. Bryce would want an explanation at some point. She couldn't put off telling him about Danny forever. She took a deep breath. But not today. Today, she had other pressing matters to attend to.

The bathroom door opened and women began to pour in, signaling that the service had let out. She exited and found Bryce standing in the foyer speaking with Cassidy and an older couple who had to be her parents.

Bryce turned to Lucy as she approached them. "Here she is. Lucy, this is Paul and Arlena Summers, Cassidy's parents. They've agreed to talk to us about when my dad was arrested."

Arlena Summers was tall and very well put together.

Not a hair was out of place; her makeup was impeccable and her clothes prim. Paul Summers, on the other hand, looked more disheveled. His clothes were wrinkled and he looked like he'd been sleeping, but of the two, he was warmer. He greeted her with a big smile and a handshake.

"We're happy to do anything we can to help these boys. We were all like family at one time," he said, giving Lucy's hand a shake that lasted a moment too long.

"My daughter tells me you'd like to ask us some questions about that nonsense that happened with Bryce's father," Mrs. Summers said. "We'll be happy to help in any way we can." Her expression, however, told a different story. She didn't like bringing up such unpleasant matters, and it showed.

"I appreciate your help," Lucy told them both.

"What would you like to know?"

"You were friends with the Tippitts, weren't you?"

Mrs. Summers answered. "Yes, Bryce's mother and I were friendly, but the men were far closer. We often spent weekends together, Sunday dinners and such. Bryce and Cassidy hit it off immediately."

Lucy turned to Mr. Summers. "So did you know he and Amanda Lake were having an affair?"

He looked taken aback by her abrupt question. He reached for her arm and took a step away from the group, lowering his voice. "It's not something we ever talked about, but he did often use me as an alibi. He would tell his wife we were going out fishing when he would actually be going to see her. I regret now that I covered for him. Had I realized how it would all turn out, I would have spoken up sooner."

"Sooner?"

"Yes, I'm the one who told the police about the affair once the young woman was found dead. They had no idea."

"So you turned your friend into the police?"

"I couldn't keep quiet, could I? Not after knowing what he'd done."

"So you believe he killed her then?"

"What other explanation is there? They were having an affair. I'd say they both got what they deserved."

That sounded harsh. "You think she deserved to die?"

"Well, she wasn't living a good life. She paid the price for it. It's tragic, but it was avoidable."

Lucy didn't like the feeling this man was giving off. No woman ever deserved to be killed, no matter what she'd done. She thanked the couple for agreeing to answer her questions, and they left, along with Cassidy.

"They're not a very compassionate couple, are they?"

"They're a complicated family."

"How so?"

"Cassidy's mom is all about looks and presenting a united front, but I don't think they've had a good marriage for years. Cassidy said things were so bad between them that she had to come here to live with her grandmother when she was in high school."

"They weren't living here?"

"No, they moved away from Whitten not too long after the murder. Mrs. Summer's job kept them moving around a lot. She finally retired a few years ago, and they moved back to town. Cassidy had already been living here."

"I'll bet she was happy to see them again."

"Like I said, it's a complicated family." He shrugged again. "Who doesn't have a complicated family history?"

She smiled at his attempt at humor. "Is there anyone else I can talk to?"

He led her to several others, elders at the church who had been there since the murder. They were more open to discussing the matter, given its possible relation to the current deaths. Some were even shocked to learn Lucy was trying to tie them together.

"That was an isolated incident," a Mr. Morgan stated. "Everyone knows John Tippitt killed the girl. If he hadn't, he wouldn't have killed himself."

Lucy saw Bryce grimace, and realized this was a terrible reminder to his own family.

"I felt sorry for you boys," a Mrs. Shields told Bryce. "You didn't ask for your lives to fall apart. Neither did your mother, only she didn't take the tragedy very well. She fell apart. I tried to counsel her to turn to the Lord, but she always felt so betrayed, not only by her husband but by God too."

Lucy was surprised to hear that, but she understood it. Bryce's father had admitted to having an affair and had been accused of killing a woman. It was a tough thing to realize you didn't know the person you loved. She understood it probably better than anyone. Then again, Bryce's mother wasn't an FBI-trained behavioral analyst.

"Did she ever forgive him?" she asked Bryce once they were alone.

"I'm sorry?"

"Your mother. Did she ever forgive your father... or God?"

He adjusted the strap on his sling nervously. "No. Once he was gone, she was forced to work two and sometimes three jobs just to pay the bills. My dad left her with a heavy burden, and she didn't bear it well. I'm sure she knew in her heart that it wasn't God who was to blame, but that bitterness takes hold, you know. To my knowledge, she never set foot in a church again, but I was away in the marines for a long time before she died."

Lucy shook her head. It amazed her that one person's actions could have such rippling consequences. It angered her too. Didn't they realize they weren't only causing problems for themselves, but for others too? Again, her mind went back to Danny and her own culpability. He'd done the crime, but she was paying the price.

"What about you?" she asked him. "Did you and Clint continue to attend church?"

"No way. Mom would never have allowed it. Everyone was looking at us and judging us. Showing our faces there wasn't something we felt we could do. Clint and I spent most Sundays alone. Some people from church did try to reach out to us and assure us that we weren't forgotten. They said they didn't blame us for what happened, but we still didn't feel comfortable attending church."

"Yet you go now. What happened?"

His face broke into a smile. "I met a man in Afghanistan. One of my teammates was very religious. He was a nice guy and everyone liked him. I noticed he spent his time reading the Bible. He always seemed so at peace no matter what was happening in his life, and I noticed that and questioned him about it. He told me his peace came from the Lord and from spending time in the Word. I'd just learned about Meghan, and was fighting with Bridgette to even get a photo of my daughter. I was ready to feel a different emotion besides anger. I blamed everyone else but myself for the bad choices I'd made in life. But I met Rhett and I wanted that peace he had so I started reading my Bible. I committed my life to the Lord."

"And what happened?"

"Well, some things got better. I finally got Meghan back. I can't say I'm happy about how it happened. She misses her mom. But it all worked out. I changed inside. I stopped blaming others for everything and finally found that peace in the Lord Rhett had told me about." He shrugged. "Now all of this with Clint is rearing its head again. I confess, it's hard to be faithful and trust that it will all work out, but hey, what else am I going to do?" He glanced at her, and she feared he would ask her about the earlier incident. Instead, he asked a simpler question. "What about you? Were you raised in church?"

She smiled, recalling her childhood faith. "My parents had us at church every time the doors were open. I accepted Christ when I was twelve, and I lived with that faith for a long time."

He glanced at her, and she swore he could see right into her soul and the big, gaping hole that now lived there. "But not anymore?"

She shrugged. "Things happen." She wasn't ready to go into the details of Danny and how she'd failed.

He didn't press her, only reached for her hand and squeezed it in a reassuring gesture. She liked that he didn't try to press her for information. It wasn't fair. She knew nearly every detail of his life, yet she kept her own hidden. That was no way to form a relationship. But did she want a relationship with this man? She glanced at him and felt her heart flutter. She did, and that made it even harder. If she got too close to him and he knew the truth about her, he wouldn't be so understanding, would he?

She liked what he'd had to say about finding that peace that surpassed all understanding. She used to know it too, back before Danny, but she didn't deserve such peace. She knew the verses and knew that God could forgive her for her failure to see Danny's shortcomings before it was too late, yet she didn't feel like she deserved that forgiveness. She had too much to make up for.

Bryce received a text message from Cassidy asking him to meet her by the back door of the church. He left Lucy speaking with a couple who'd known Amanda Lake well while he hurried to meet her. Cassidy wouldn't have texted him if it wasn't important, but he wondered why she couldn't tell him what she had to say a few minutes ago when they'd been speaking with her and her parents.

When he saw her, her arms were folded and she was shaking her head at him. He owed her big-time, yet he saw disapproval in her expression.

"You're getting too close to that woman," she finally said as he approached her.

"What do you mean?"

She poked him in the chest with her finger. "You know exactly what I mean, Bryce Tippitt. She's FBI. She's law enforcement, and worst of all, she works for the government. When have they ever been a friend to your family?"

That last part stung, but she wasn't saying anything he hadn't thought before. He recalled the meeting with his supervisor at SOA telling him the government would no longer be needing his services. They'd used him, and then when he and his team had sullied their reputation, they'd cut him loose without another thought. The media had hailed them as heroes, but his own government had set him aside like he didn't matter. It was the story of his life. He hadn't mattered to his mother, he hadn't mattered to the mother of his child and he hadn't mattered to his own government.

His heart told him Lucy was different. Yes, she was government, but she was also a beautiful, intelligent woman. His mind warned him to be careful.

"You don't see it, do you?" Cassidy asked, pulling him back to the present.

"What?"

"She's getting close to you so she can get closer to Clint. She came to town with one mission, Bryce. To uncover the identity of the serial killer. She's only getting close to you to gather intel about Clint."

He shrugged off her concern. "I don't believe that."

"It doesn't matter what you believe. That woman is a danger to this family. She's a danger to you and to Meghan."

"How? She's doing her job. She's stopping a serial killer. How can that be wrong?"

"What's going to happen to Meghan when she arrests Clint for those murders, Bryce? Her life will be over. She'll be ostracized. She'll forever be known as the niece of a killer. What kind of life will she have after that? Who'll want to marry her? What college will she get into? Who'll want to hire her?"

He knew firsthand the consequences Cassidy was talking about. He'd lived them himself, although his father had only been accused of killing one woman. This maniac was a serial killer. "But Clint is not a killer."

"I know that and you know that, but this Agent Sanderson is here looking for blood. She has to find this guy. They're like bloodhounds. They get a scent, and they attack it until they kill something and bring it home. Right now, the local police have given her Clint's scent. She has to make some progress or it'll cost her her reputation."

"Lucy wouldn't do that. She wouldn't falsify evidence."

"She doesn't have to. All she has to do is write up a profile that fits your brother. Think about it. She's cozying up to you, Bryce, and you're pouring your heart out to her about Clint and what he's truly like. I've read up on behavioral science. She doesn't have to name a suspect. She only has to point the way, and you and I both know Chief Dobson only wants this profile as one more nail in Clint's coffin." She reached out for his arm, and her face held sympathy for him. "Bryce, you know how much I care about you and Meghan. You've got to think about her. What if the police are right and

Clint isn't who you think he is? You've got to protect your daughter."

"From Clint?"

"From the truth. From the fallout of his arrest."

"No." He shook his head. "I know my brother isn't evil. Besides, I could never ignore something like that if I knew about it. How could I justify keeping that kind of secret if it meant someone got away with murder? If it meant more people's lives were in danger." He waved his hand. "No, no. I couldn't live with myself. If they ever find solid evidence against Clint, I don't know what I'll do, but I won't hide it and I won't protect him."

She sighed. "You're right, of course. I was only thinking about Meghan and how this is all affecting her."

"I know you were, and I appreciate that. I'm glad she's got someone like you watching out for her."

She took a step toward him. "It's not only her back I'm watching, Bryce. I'm here for you too."

He reached for her hand and squeezed it. She looked disappointed in the gesture, but it was all he could give her. He was being insensitive talking to her about Lucy when he knew she had her own feelings for him, feelings that he'd never been able to reciprocate. He'd never seen her as anything more than a friend, and he doubted he ever would. But he was glad she would always be his friend.

SIX

Lucy could see the morning's outing had taken more out of Bryce than he wanted to admit, so once they returned to his house, she enlisted Meghan's help to convince him to take another pain pill and rest. At his daughter's insistence, he reluctantly complied.

Once he was asleep, Lucy messaged Detective Ross to update him on the interviews she'd conducted this morning with Amanda Lake's acquaintances. When he responded he was about to view security footage from her attack at the hotel, she charged Meghan with looking out for her father, then borrowed Bryce's truck and drove to town. She wanted to be there when Ross examined that footage and hopefully discover who was targeting her.

She met him at the precinct, and he keyed up the video surveillance tape he'd gotten from the hotel.

"The hotel staff was able to identify everyone coming and going in the footage except for one person. This guy." He stopped the tape at an image of someone leaving the hotel through the back door. The suspect was dressed in black and wearing a baseball cap to hide his face. He was tall but slender, and something about the image didn't sit right with Lucy.

"Do you recognize him?"

"No. How could I? You can't even see his face. But go back several seconds. Our guy passed by another man in the hallway." Ross keyed that image back up, and Lucy knew she was right. "Look how much larger the other man is compared to our guy. And look at the way he walks. I'm not sure that's a man at all, Detective Ross. I think we're looking for a woman."

He stared at the image, then leaned back in his chair and heaved a sigh. "I think you might be right."

"A woman could have set up that trap as easily as a man. Plus it might explain why someone is after me when I haven't done anything to anyone."

"Do you think she's working with the Back Roads Killer?"

"Nothing in his profile suggests he would have a partner. The type of violence he perpetrates screams a hatred for women. But it is possible there's someone in his life who is submissive to him, and he's forcing her to do his bidding. It would have to be someone very close to him, a wife or significant other, or a close family member—someone trapped in the relationship with this killer. Most people who discovered their family member or friend was a killer would be too horrified to participate in any wrongdoings, so this would have be someone he has control over or who has something to lose if his deeds are uncovered."

"Okay, so we go back to the realization that if she kills an FBI agent, the town will be swarming with federal agents determined to hunt down the killer."

"What if she's not trying to cover his tracks? What if she's trying to get him captured?"

"An anonymous tip would be the easiest way to accomplish that, not murder," Ross stated.

"This woman, if it is a woman, would be so beaten down by this secret looming over her life. She's trapped, and she can't take any risks that he'll discover she had a hand in turning him in. He's sent her to take care of me, but if she botches the job, she knows we'll be looking into it."

"Or she just wants to kill you to stop you from investigating and isn't thinking about the consequences."

She glanced at the image on the screen and realized Detective Ross was right. She hadn't botched the booby trap in the hotel bathroom. Lucy had only escaped that because Bryce had gotten to the door first. She hated to think there was someone out there willing to kill her to keep the identity of a serial murderer safe. But then again, she'd witnessed women commit terrible acts in the name of love.

"Did you get my message about the updated age of the suspect?"

"I did and I see the similarities. I can't believe someone didn't put that together sooner. But why the gap between killings? Do you think he's been in prison?"

"Possibly."

"I'll have records pulled to see if we have anyone recently released from prison who's now living in the area, see if they lived here twenty years ago."

"It's also possible he was living elsewhere during those years. He may have simply moved away from the area after the first murder. I'll check with the FBI database to see if we can find any similar deaths across the country. If he continued killing, we may be able to track his movements through the years."

His phone buzzed and he groaned. "The chief wants to see us."

She found it odd that the chief of police was working on a Sunday afternoon, but she figured she knew the reason he wanted to see her. "Did you tell him about the update in my profile?"

"I did. I updated him this morning."

Just as she thought. She felt like a student being sent to the principal's office for being tardy or insubordinate, but she knew he was unhappy with the direction her investigation was taking. At least she wasn't going in alone.

"I'm glad you're both here this afternoon," the chief said as they entered his office. "I wanted to speak to you, Agent Sanderson, but when I arrived at the office, I found we'd received the results back on what was inside the syringe the killer tried to inject you with."

He handed her the sheet of paper with the lab results, and she quickly scanned it. "Socoline. I've heard of it. That's a powerful anesthetic that causes short-term paralysis. It may be the key to uncovering this perpetrator if we can figure out where he's getting the drugs from. We need to check with all hospitals, veterinarian clinics, pharmacies to find out if anyone has a problem with missing drugs. We should also reach out to any government agencies who might have an ongoing investigation close to our area. Hospitals and pharmacies are required to report missing inventory. If we can find this, it may be the lead we've been looking for."

Detective Ross took the paper from her. "I'll start reaching out to these places."

It was another piece of the puzzle they had because she'd escaped him. None of the other victims had traces of any drug in their system, but it had obviously been gone after days of captivity, which meant he only used the drugs for the initial attack. Once he'd taken them back to wherever he held them, he had a system in place to keep them incapacitated.

Excitement rushed through her. This might be the break they'd use to capture this guy.

Why did her mind go to Bryce? Should she call him and tell him about this new development? She shook her head. She would have to ask him about his brother's connection to any place to get drugs. Of course, if he didn't have any prescribed ones, there were always the illegal means. This wouldn't clear him, especially not with several drug arrests already under his belt and in the system. The local police would argue that he knew how to obtain what he needed from the streets. But even street criminals were wary of killers, at least the kinds of killers who preyed on women in the dark of night. Perhaps someone would come forward, or they would be able to trace the drug back to a certain manufacturer.

Lucy watched Detective Ross leave. She turned to face Chief Dobson, and her excitement dwindled.

She could see by the weariness on his face and the way his shoulders slumped that he was frustrated and looking for another option. He took a seat behind his desk, leaned back and sighed, locking eyes with her. "We have a problem, Agent Sanderson. It seems to me you're trying to exclude our best suspect with your profile."

So Detective Ross had indeed told him about her belief that the killer was at least forty years of age. "I'm not doing anything of the sort, Chief. I'm only going where the facts take me. There's no doubt in my mind that Amanda Lake's murder is tied to this case, and Clint Tippitt was only a child when she was killed. We are looking for an older offender. I'm certain of it."

"Unless it's a copycat killing. Who would know better than Clint how his father killed that girl? He's picking up where his father left off."

"That's quite an assumption, considering there is absolutely no physical or behavioral evidence that links Clint Tippitt to the last three murders. And I haven't seen anything in the case files to suggest a copycat killer. But the only way to know conclusively is to match the samples collected during the Amanda Lake investigation. If they match samples taken from the current case, we'll know for certain."

"We can't do that. The evidence in that case is gone."

Frustration bit at her. It wasn't uncommon for cold case evidence to disappear, but it was a tough blow. "What happened to it?"

"A tornado hit the storage unit where we used to house evidence six years ago. Those samples you refer to were lost."

And with them, the only definitive way of linking the cases. "Surely you must see the similarities between the Amanda Lake case and the current killings. How can you deny these were committed by the same man?" She saw the frustration on his face. "I'm not trying to derail your investigation, Chief. I sincerely believe there's not enough evidence in the Jessica Nelson case to even tie it in with the other cases. There's no body, and this offender has shown that displaying his victims is a signature of his. He wants to be able to show the world that he controls these women. Jessica's case is missing that huge detail. Without the body, there's simply no way to connect her case with the others. In addition, her disappearance took place a year and a half before the next woman vanished and was murdered. The other killings were only four to six months apart. That's an enormous gap, further evidence that it can't be tied to the others."

"I want you to adjust your findings to include the Nelson girl."

"That would mean compromising everything I stand for in behavioral analysis."

"Don't you understand that without it, a killer may go free?"

She saw his dilemma. He was desperately trying to find justice, but Lucy was more certain than ever that he was looking in the wrong direction. "I understand that your case against Clint Tippitt falls apart without Jessica Nelson's case tying them together. Maybe, just maybe, there's a reason for that, Chief."

"If I have to, I'll call your supervisor and tell him to change it."

"You can certainly try that, Chief, but you'll find my team back at the Behavioral Analysis Unit supports one another. If you'd like, I can offer to have a colleague re-evaluate my findings. If, after that, they find some discrepancies, we can all address them together."

He tapped nervously on his desk. "Does this have

anything to do with how close you and Bryce Tippitt have gotten lately?"

She felt her face redden, but she couldn't decide if it was due to anger or embarrassment. How dare he accuse her of being biased? She tried very hard not to be. But at the same time, wasn't that the very fear that concerned her too—having her emotions clouded by her own feelings for Bryce? Wasn't that why she'd pushed him away when all she wanted to do was fall into his embrace?

"I'll contact my supervisor and ask him to have someone evaluate my profile. It's the best I can do for now, Chief, but when it comes back saying the same thing as me, what will you do then? Will you continue your quest to arrest an innocent man of murder?"

"He's not innocent."

"I can't speak to his involvement in Jessica Nelson's disappearance, but I believe wholeheartedly he was not involved in the rape and murders of the last three victims."

"And that's based on your expert opinion, is it?"

"Yes, it is. He simply doesn't fit the profile, and there is no inciting factor in his life that instigated these killings."

"None that you're aware of."

"Well, none that have been brought forward by this task force. If you have other information you haven't shared with me, I'd be happy to reevaluate my profile."

He wasn't pleased with her decision, but he had no choice but to accept it. "That'll be all, Agent Sanderson."

She stood to leave, but then stopped and turned back

to him. "Why are you so intent on believing Clint Tippitt is the killer?"

He looked up and locked eyes with her. "I know that family much better than you do, Lucy."

She'd read in the case file that the chief had been the responding officer to the Lake case. It must have haunted him knowing that she had never received justice.

As she walked, she pulled out her phone and dialed the office. She didn't like having her work questioned, yet she had similar concerns. There would have been a time when her confidence in her work would have been unquestioned, or at least she wouldn't have doubted herself, but that wasn't now. Danny had changed all that. Now, having her work questioned sent her confidence spiraling downward.

It wouldn't hurt to have someone double-check her profile. She didn't like asking though. It made her look as weak and unconfident as she felt. But she made the call and hung up feeling even worse than after she'd spoken to the chief. She hated the doubt that clung to her. Her supervisor had sent her here to try to get her confidence back, but she wasn't sure that would ever happen. Still, could she risk letting a killer go free because of her issues?

She grabbed her notes and headed outside, anxious to get back to the house and check on Bryce, but she stopped short when she approached the truck.

Bryce was leaning against it waiting for her.

"I woke up and you were gone." He adjusted the strap on his sling. "I don't like being excluded, Lucy."

"How did you get here?" She had his truck and hadn't seen another car at his house.

"I took a cab."

"I was just coming back to check on you. How's your arm?"

"It's fine. It doesn't even hurt."

She doubted that. His face seemed flush, and he'd given a slight grimace when he fidgeted with the sling. "Get in. I'll take you back home, and I promise I won't leave again without telling you."

He locked eyes with her. "I'm holding you to that promise."

He slipped into the passenger's seat while she drove, heading toward his ranch. She was in the middle of telling him about all they'd discovered this afternoon when she pressed on the brakes to slow down around a sharp curve, and the pedal went right to the floor.

She pressed it again. Nothing happened. The brakes weren't working.

"What's wrong?" Bryce asked, seeing her frantic motions.

"The brakes are out." She pushed on the emergency brake, but it was too late. They rounded the curve too sharply and the truck spun out of control. She noted Bryce bracing as they spun through the guardrail and plummeted into the river below.

The truck hit the water with a thud. The seat belt jerked her around, then jarred her as the vehicle hit the water. Her head slammed against the window, and the drop into the river knocked the breath from her lungs. She expected the vehicle to sink, but it didn't right away. It floated for half a second, then water began to seep in.

Bryce pulled the sling over his head and tossed it, unbuckled his seat belt, then reached over and unbuckled Lucy's.

"We have to get out of here."

She pushed at her door, but the weight against it was too great. "It won't budge." She tried the power windows. Nothing happened.

"Once the water rises over the doors, we should be able to push them open."

Oh God, please help us!

"We have to stay together," Bryce said. "When the truck submerges completely, hold on to me. The currents will try to pull us apart, but we have to make it to the riverbank."

She nodded. She'd been through training at the academy and had even been in shoot-outs, but this was different. Her insides were quivering with fear, and the sound of her own heartbeat hammered in her ears.

Water pressed at the windshield, causing minibreaks that would eventually shatter it. When it did, the cold water would be like knives stabbing her all over. Bryce pushed the door open and swam out, pulling her along behind him. She did her best to push through the water to keep up with him, but her hand slipped and he disappeared. The currents were strong and pulled her down. She fought and struggled to reach the light at the top.

She probably deserved this after failing to notice Danny's substance abuse. Her failure had killed a family, and if this was her punishment, then that should be okay. She should be okay with it. But she wasn't. She wanted to live. Dying here was not in her plans.

Her lungs screamed for air, but she wouldn't give

up. She pushed and struggled, focused on the light at the top.

Suddenly arms surrounded her, and she was pinned down. She spun to see Bryce slipping his arms around her waist. He was pulling her the other way. She struggled against him, fear pulsing through her and the light moving farther and farther away. She struggled against him, but he was stronger and easily pulled her along with him. Her lungs were filling with acid, and she couldn't hold her breath for one second longer. She gasped for breath and took in water, choking and frozen. It seemed like an eternity passed while she choked and gurgled, but the strong arms pulling her along never loosened.

And she knew one thing as she lost consciousness. Her death wouldn't settle the score for what she'd done.

Bryce ignored the pain screaming from his shoulder and burst through the water, pulling Lucy along with him. She'd taken in water and lost consciousness before they reached the surface. He'd panicked when her hand had slipped from his, especially when he realized she was swimming back down toward the headlights of the sinking truck. She would have drowned for certain if he hadn't found her. She might still.

He couldn't think of that now. There was nothing to do for her until they reached the bank. He swam as hard as he could and silently thanked God when they reached the edge of the river. He pulled her up onto the rocks and then lifted her head and started CPR to release the water in her lungs. His mind was numb, counting out the things he needed to do to revive her.

His training had prepared him for this day, and he was able to remain composed and do what he needed to do, but somewhere beneath the mechanical techniques of CPR, his mind was swirling.

He didn't want her to die, and not only because it would seal the fate of his brother, but because he liked her smile and determination, and he liked the way Meghan had reacted to her. For the first time in a long time, he'd seen the hope for something more permanent in their future, for a motherly figure for his daughter and a helpmate for him. Maybe it wouldn't be her, but she'd certainly set the spark that might make it possible one day.

She gasped and water spouted from her mouth. He turned her over to clear her lungs and allow the water to drain out. She was breathing again—that was good.

"Wh-what happened?"

He stared up at the busted guardrail and shook his head. "Just an accident. We're okay now."

She nodded and lay back, still breathing heavily. The evening air was cool, and the water had been freezing. They needed to get out of their clothes and get warm. If they stayed here, they would quickly succumb to hypothermia.

He checked his pockets for his phone. It was gone, probably floating in the river somewhere. "Did your phone survive?"

She shook her head. "No, it was in my bag." Which was also at the bottom of the river, presumably.

So they were stranded on the riverbank on a cold night with no way to communicate with anyone. "We have to get up to the road."

"I can make it," she insisted, although she didn't look like she could. She was shaking from the chill and favoring her previously injured ankle.

His own shoulder was screaming in pain, and he noticed some blood on his shirt. He recalled Cassidy telling him to keep it dry. Well, it wasn't like he'd chosen to get it wet.

Lucy squared her shoulders and started climbing, reaching for anything, a tree root or grounded bush that could help her up the steep embankment. He followed behind, watching her footsteps so the soft dirt wouldn't give beneath her. As they neared the top, her foot slipped and she fell into his arms. He held her a moment too long, remembering the fear that had gripped him when her hand had slipped from his, before she turned back.

She started climbing again and scrambled to the top. She reached back, grabbed his hand and helped pull him over the edge.

"What do we do now?" she asked.

"My house is less than a mile down the road. We should start walking."

As they walked, he wrapped his arm around her to break the chill that burst through them both. Lucy didn't argue. She leaned against him, shivering, her shoulders quivering from the wet clothes and chill in the air.

"I—I can't go anymore," she said, stopping. "I need to rest."

"No, we have to keep moving." Stopping now would be too dangerous—hypothermia would set in.

Headlights shone against the trees ahead of him, and he spun around to see a car approaching.

Thank You, God.

He stepped into the road and flagged down the car. It pulled to the side of the road and stopped. The door opened and Cassidy got out.

"What happened?" She ran to him and took in his drenched state, then noticed his wound bleeding.

"The truck went over the rail. We went into the river."

She glanced behind him at Lucy as shock and horror flooded her face. "We need to get you someplace warm. Get in the car." She ran to the passenger's side and opened the door. Bryce helped Lucy inside, then climbed into the back seat.

"Take us to my house."

"You need to go to the hospital." She dialed 911 as she drove and alerted them to the situation. When they arrived at the emergency room, a group was waiting to treat them.

Cassidy led Bryce into one area while Lucy was taken to another.

At the hospital, Bryce grew restless. He'd had his bandage changed and an IV inserted for fluids but was deemed otherwise in good shape after their ordeal. He was ready to get out of there and check on Lucy. Despite her determination and grit, she'd grown pale and weak once they were out of danger. He wanted to know how she was.

"Bryce, what are you doing?"

He turned to find Cassidy at the door. Anger was written all over her expression. "What were you doing in that truck, Bryce? I talked to Meghan earlier and you were sleeping. What happened?"

"I woke up and Lucy had left, so I went to find her. We were driving back to the ranch when the brakes failed."

"You risked your life to save her?"

"Of course. I couldn't leave her to drown."

She shook her head. "You have a family to think about, Bryce. You can't take those kinds of risks."

"What was I supposed to do? Let her drown? It was a good thing you came upon us. What were you doing out that way?"

"I was coming to your house. I was going to cook you and Meghan supper." She pulled a needle from her pocket and injected it into his IV.

"What's that?"

"Something to help you rest."

"No, I have to check on Lucy."

He tried to sit up, but she pushed him back down. "No, you need your rest. You haven't even recovered from being shot."

He reached for her hand as the medicine she'd given him began to work. "Thank you, Cassidy. You're a good friend."

"You're my best friend, Bryce. You have been since we were kids. I'll always be here for you."

They were the last words he heard her say before he drifted off to sleep, but when he awoke, they were still on his mind. He was thankful to have a friend like Cassidy. She'd been right about him needing rest. He did feel better, and his arm wasn't hurting like before, but he had no idea how long he'd been asleep. It was still nighttime, as evidenced by the bright lights and dark sky outside the window.

Cassidy had been his best friend for as long as he could remember. It had been Cassidy who'd alerted him about Bridgette's pregnancy and that he had a daughter when Meghan's mom hid the pregnancy and birth from him, and Cassidy who had stood by him through the custody battles. She'd even been there for Meghan, helping her adjust to her new living arrangements after Bridgette's death, and she'd made the transition easier for them all. He owed Cassidy more than he could ever repay her. But for right now, he had to make sure Lucy was okay.

He pulled out his IV, slid off the hospital bed, then headed down the hallway looking for Lucy's room. He finally found it. He knocked, then walked inside when she replied to come in. She looked small and frail on the all-white hospital bed, but her hair cascaded against the stark white of the sheets and blanket. Her eyes lit up when she spotted him.

"Bryce, I'm so glad to see you. I was worried. Are you okay?"

"I'm fine. Cassidy gave me something to make me sleep, but I'm better now. How are you?"

"I'm okay. It's all still a blur what happened, but I know I owe you my life. You saved me."

"You were disoriented. It's not uncommon."

"I was sure I was heading for the surface. I can't believe how turned around I was. Thank you."

Another knock came on the door, and Chief Dobson entered. He spotted Bryce. "I'm glad you're here. I checked your room first and saw you weren't there. I was hoping you two were together."

It had been hours since he'd given his statement to the police about the accident. He glanced at the clock and realized he'd slept for six hours.

"We pulled your truck from the water and had it towed to a local garage. You both said in your statements that the brakes failed. Billy Mason had a preliminary look at them." He stopped and looked at Bryce. "The brake line was deliberately cut."

Lucy gasped. "Are you sure?"

"Billy said it was too clean to be accidental. Whoever did it couldn't have known you would have gone over that rail, but they did intend for you to crash. This was no accident."

Bryce lowered himself into a chair at this revelation. He glanced at Lucy and saw the same confusion and understanding on her face. Someone had targeted her again. This attack had been planned and premeditated.

"We need to narrow down the window when it could have happened. When was the last time you drove your pickup prior to yesterday afternoon?"

Bryce looked at her and tried to retrace their steps. "We drove it to church yesterday morning, then back to the house."

"Then I took it to the police station. I was there all afternoon. Bryce took a cab to the station, and we headed back to his place. They were working fine when I drove it into town."

According to Meghan, Lucy had been gone for three hours before he awoke. A three-hour window when someone had to know where that truck was parked and that she would be the one driving it.

Whoever was targeting her wasn't taking chances. He was watching her movements and knew where she'd been.

Lucy was anxious to get back to work after her ordeal in the water. She'd come too close to dying this time, and the fear had her rattled. She couldn't shake off the feeling that maybe she was getting what she deserved after missing all the clues about Danny's addiction. Was this the price she had to pay for her part in the death of the Williams family?

A verse from the Bible came to her. Micah 7:19: *He will turn again, He will have compassion upon us; He will subdue our iniquities; and thou wilt cast all their sins into the depths of the sea.*

Her brother had steered her toward that verse after Danny's death, and it had stayed with her. She liked the part about God tossing her sins into the depths of the sea and subduing her iniquities. But could He really do it? Was it saying that God would no longer think upon what she'd done or what she'd failed to do? She'd heard that somewhere and wanted to believe it, but how could He forget when she never could?

She closed her eyes and took a deep breath, trying to envision tossing her guilt and shame into the ocean and watching it sink to the bottom. She liked the idea, but she saw herself clearly pulling on the line, pulling it back to the top. She wouldn't let it go, and that was the problem. How could God ever forgive and forget when no one else could? When she couldn't?

The image of the water reminded her of the river, and she shuddered. She and Bryce had nearly been dropped to the bottom themselves. Someone wanted her out of the way, and she was no closer to uncovering who it was.

She turned back to her notes and tried to make sense of everything she'd learned about this case so far. There had to be something she was missing, but she couldn't put her finger on it yet. Someone wanted her dead, and no one around her was safe until she discovered who.

She was more convinced than ever that Amanda Lake had been the first victim of the Back Roads Killer, and that by digging into her life, she would uncover something that would lead her to the killer.

She read through the notes she'd jotted down about the conversations she'd had with the Summerses. Cassidy's father had confessed that John Tippitt had used their fishing trips as an alibi for his rendezvous with his mistress, but something about his statement struck her as odd.

She dug through the files until she found Amanda Lake's and opened it on the bed. She searched through the witness statements and found one the police had taken from Paul twenty years ago during the initial investigation. Back then, he'd told the police he'd known about his friend's indiscretions but that he'd often used hunting trips, not fishing trips, as his alibi. Why had he said hunting trips back then but fishing trips now? It was a small detail, but it stood out to her.

So Paul had lied to cover for his friend's infidelity. Could she take anything from that? It wasn't so unusual, but how had he felt when his friend was accused of murdering Amanda Lake?

She put the file away and realized she was putting her own shame and guilt on him. It wasn't her business how he'd felt. Any normal person would have been justifiably horrified when the truth came out. He was probably carrying around the same shame and guilt for covering for Bryce's dad as she was still carrying for Danny. The only difference was she hadn't been covering for him intentionally. She'd had no idea about his drug use. She still struggled with realizing she hadn't seen it. There must have been clues she'd overlooked. She didn't think she'd done so on purpose. She couldn't point to anything now that she'd known about. But there must have been something she hadn't seen or had chosen not to see. And that was the hardest part to her. She didn't think she had, but she must have known on some level. People didn't hide that kind of behavior very well, did they? And besides, it was her job to discover if they did.

The conference room door opened and Detective Ross walked in. Tension poured off him. "Something has happened. He tried to grab another woman. She managed to escape."

Lucy held her breath as relief flowed over her. At least he wouldn't claim another victim.

"There's something else," he said. "She was able to lead officers to a shack in the woods. We think it's where he kept his victims. I'm heading out to the scene now if you want to come."

"I do." Lucy hurried to follow him as excitement rushed through her. If they had indeed located the killer's hideout, they were another step closer to discovering his identity.

SEVEN

She rode with Detective Ross to the scene. When he turned onto the dirt road, panic gripped her, a call-back to the fear this turn-off had caused her while she was trapped inside that trunk. She closed her eyes and tried to breathe and tamp down the panic that was rising inside her, but the familiar bumps in the road made that difficult.

"You okay?" Detective Ross asked her.

"I'm fine." She concentrated on her breathing. She had to get a grip, but it was difficult because her head was spinning. Everything seemed to be culminating at this moment, and she was having a difficult time compartmentalizing all that had happened to her.

She was thankful when he pulled the car to a stop behind a group of police cruisers, the forensic team's van and the chief's SUV.

Lucy got out and saw a small cabin-like structure they were surrounding. Forensic teams were already coming and going, and officers were snapping photographs and taking measurements.

She spotted Chief Dobson, who approached her.

"Looks like this was the place he kept them. I've got people inside collecting evidence now. It's an evidence gold mine in there."

"What about the victim?"

"She's been transported to the hospital, but she seems unhurt. Like you, she was able to escape him, but she was more familiar with the area and able to tell officers where she'd been taken. By the time they arrived, the perpetrator was long gone, but this is definitely his place."

She nodded. "I'd like to see inside."

"Are you sure you want to do that? He was probably taking you to this place when you escaped."

"Which is why I need to see it." Her gut clenched. As a victim, she didn't want to know what was inside that cabin, but as a profiler, she needed to see. She couldn't close her eyes to this man's methods if they ever hoped to hunt him down. Because, regardless of how flippant she'd found the chief's statement, this kill shed was a key location in their efforts to catch a serial killer. "Any idea who owns this place?"

"No, it's been abandoned for years. Anyone could have come upon it and done the repairs to it."

She pulled on a pair of latex gloves so she wouldn't corrupt the scene with her fingerprints, then stepped inside. It was small, but there was already a team in there gathering forensic evidence. The windows were blackened out with what looked like paint, with only a small section scratched off. That must have been for him to see outside in case someone came along. One forensic tech ran a light over the floor and found traces of blood. A table along one wall held a row of tools, and another black light also showed traces of blood on them.

A pair of heavy iron chains in a corner were bolted to a wall, and a pit had been dug. This was where he kept them prisoner. This cabin was so far out in the woods, no one would hear their screams.

Terror rushed through her at how close she'd come to being here. If she hadn't acted when she did, or if he'd caught up with her in the woods, she would have been stuck in this pit, chained up and helpless.

Suddenly, everything came crashing down around her. The multiple attacks, nearly drowning and even the feel of Bryce's arms around her as he pulled her to safety. It had all started because of this monster. She'd come here to capture him, yet he'd been torturing her since the moment she'd arrived in town.

She couldn't catch her breath. She needed out of this cabin, and fast. She hurried for the door and maneuvered her way past a group of officers to the edge of the trees. She knelt, her heart racing at the memory of how close she'd come to being the killer's next victim. Never to see her family and friends again. Never to breathe fresh air again. At the mercy of a maniac with sharp tools and a diabolical determination to make her suffer.

She closed her eyes and concentrated on her breathing as panic threatened her. *Breathe in. Breathe out. Concentrate on the air filling your lungs.* Finally her heart rate slowed and her mind stopped spinning. She glanced up. The scene had continued on without her, but now she had to go back inside and be less personal with her observations. This couldn't be a place where she'd almost died. She had to force herself to see it only as a place to be profiled. It was the only way she was going to catch a killer.

"We're getting to him, Bryce," Lucy said when she called him later that day. "He's feeling the pressure. Plus I've just received a call from my supervisor. So far they've located six other states with unsolved murders matching our killer's MO. Until further evidence is uncovered to dispute it, they are assuming it's the same killer. This guy has definitely been around for a while. We're going to hold a press conference to address what we've found."

He heard the excitement in her voice over the phone and wished he was there with her, but their encounter in the river had taken a greater toll on him than it had on her. His shoulder had taken the brunt of it, and she'd insisted he stay home to rest. He'd given in only because his body was protesting, and he'd assumed she would simply be going over files at the precinct today.

Of course, this would be the day when a break came in the case, when he wasn't there.

"Are you sure that's the right thing to do?" To him, a press conference sounded like she was placing a target on herself, as if she didn't already have one.

"Don't you see? He's feeling the pressure. He failed to abduct another woman, and now he knows we've found his kill shed and all his tools. We've already crippled him. He'll be struggling right now and he'll want to lash out, but he'll have to hold himself back because we have all his killing tools. We need to strike now, to add more pressure to him by going on television and telling the world how crippled he is. That added pressure will eventually make him snap."

"Doesn't that mean he'll come after you?"

"He already is. I've become the focus of his rage. I'm the one he's identified as the person who can bring him down. Since I came to town, he's lost everything. Not only am I the one who got away, I'm also the one responsible for bringing down his sanctuary. He's on the edge. Now, we just have to push him over it. Someone will notice it, and that may be the person who calls us with the information that leads us to capture this guy once and for all."

He hoped she was right, but she was the professional and he trusted her judgment. He only wished he was there to be by her side and keep her safe, but he was in no condition to do so today. If only they would wait until tomorrow, until he could get his strength back. But this killer had already tried to abduct another woman. He might try again, and this time, his victim might not escape with her life.

He also didn't like the idea that he couldn't get ahold of his brother. She talked about him feeling the pressure. Clint had been spiraling downward for a while. Bryce hadn't even been able to tell him yet that Lucy's profile exonerated him, at least for the murders of the last three victims. How odd was it that the murder his father had been accused of would be the thing to exonerate Clint?

He gazed at the bookshelf that held his family's photos, scanning pictures from a recent one of Meghan and her horse, Charlie, to a long-ago shot of him and Clint with their mom and dad, from a time when they were a happy family. Back before the deaths and accusations that had tainted this family.

His father had never denied the affair, but he had vehemently denied killing Amanda Lake. He'd loved her. He'd confessed that much to Bryce. Such a weight for an eleven-year-old's shoulders. Too much weight, he knew. He would never lay such heavy information on Meghan's shoulders. One more indication that his parents had lost the ability to shield their children from the harsh realities of their own grief and suffering. His mother hadn't been much better. She'd been humiliated for all the world to see. Then she'd been saddled with being a single mother. Some women rose to the challenge. She hadn't. She'd struggled, scrimped and saved to keep a roof over their heads, and had soon seen her boys as a burden she'd been saddled with, becoming angry and bitter until her dying day.

Bryce had never seen parenthood as a burden, but then again he'd never been through what she had. He'd tried to forgive her, tried to see her side, but the older he got, the harder time he had understanding her. He'd made it a point to fight for Meghan the moment he knew about her. He never wanted his daughter to wonder if he cared for her or believe she wasn't worthy of his love. He would never put her through what he'd been through.

It had never been his intention to take her away from her mother, despite the fact that was exactly what she had done to him, but that was life. He hadn't wanted Meghan's mother to die, but it had been a relief that the fighting was over and Meghan was his without argument. It wasn't how he'd wanted it to go, but he'd made the best of it and he hoped Meghan knew that.

He turned the television on at noon and watched the press conference. Chief Dobson introduced Lucy as an FBI profiler in town to help them, and she started going through what they'd already uncovered of the killer's profile.

Man, she was beautiful, and her loveliness shone through the television. But she was also a tough woman, as he'd come to realize. She wasn't going to be pushed around, and he liked that about her too.

"We are closing in on this killer," Lucy said into the camera. "We don't yet know his identity, but it's only a matter of time before we find him. This person will be forty to sixty years of age. He'll have a very controlling nature, but he'll also be agitated from his most recent failures to abduct two women, including myself. He also has a female in his life that we believe he's forcing into helping him. Please, if that's you, we ask that you come forward. We can help you find a way out of this. Also, we're asking the public to look for anyone who might be acting strangely. His routines have been disrupted, and he'll be stressed out. If you recognize anyone who matches this profile, please contact the police."

"Wow, she's got you wrapped around her little finger, hasn't she?"

Bryce turned and saw his brother standing in the doorway. How had he not heard him drive up or come inside? He quickly shut off the television, realizing that Clint was talking about Lucy.

"I don't know what you mean." But he didn't like the insinuation.

"She's got you duped, that's what I mean."

"Who? Lucy? I don't know what you're talking

about. Where have you been anyway? I thought we talked about communicating. You haven't taken my calls in days."

"What did you want to tell me? That the police are closing in on the killer? Why would I want to be around for that? So they can arrest me again?"

"But Lucy is proving you didn't kill those women."

"Of course I didn't kill them." He slammed the door and walked inside, pacing like a caged tiger. "Look, I'm grateful she's doing that. I truly am. But Bryce, don't you get that I'll always be known as the man who killed Jessica? I'll never live that down." He rubbed his face and groaned. "No matter what I do, no matter where I go, I'll always be seen as something I'm not. I didn't hurt her. I loved her. I wasn't always the best guy and I have a lot of regrets when I think about how I treated her sometimes, but I did not kill her."

He heard the torture in his brother's voice. What was worse? Losing the love of your life? Or being blamed for her death? "I believe you, Clint. I always have believed you."

Clint stared at him, then shook his head, confusion clouding his expression. "Why? Why do you believe me when everyone else is convinced I did it?"

It was a question people had been asking him for years, but his confidence in his brother had never wavered. "I just do. I know you've had your problems, Clint, but you're a good person. I've always known that. We're brothers. We have to stick together. You're innocent, and I know Lucy can prove that." He'd meant what he'd told Lucy about seeing evil, and he didn't see any in his brother.

But Clint was having a harder time believing it. "How can you trust her so much? She's a cop, Bryce. She's determined to hold someone responsible, and we already know the lengths the cops will go to, to close a case."

"I know the locals have tried to make a case against you—"

"I'm not talking about the case against me."

"Then what are you talking about?"

"Dad. You don't really think he killed that woman, do you? He was set up."

Clint's distrust of the police was understandable, but he wasn't old enough to remember much about that time. He hadn't been the one their father had trusted with the confession about his affair. Yet he was the one who'd believed in him all these years. He'd been the one to believe in their father's innocence...and he'd been right. If Lucy was correct, their father was innocent of Amanda Lake's murder, and Clint had believed in him all along.

He had to admit that calling in Lucy had been a last resort because he didn't trust the local police to be objective. Yes, she was government, but he trusted her. He'd been wary of trusting anyone for years. He'd been betrayed not only by the women in his life but also by his own government, yet Lucy had easily slipped through his guard. His brother simply didn't know her like Bryce did.

"I'll agree to keep an open mind about Lucy," he told his brother, "if you agree to keep the lines of communication open. I need to know where you are."

Clint's eyes hardened. "Why? I thought you believed in me."

"I do, but each time a woman goes missing and you have no alibi, it doesn't help your case."

He shook his head. "I don't care about that. I shouldn't have to prove myself to anyone." He vanished upstairs, then returned a while later with a bag of clothes.

"Where are you going?"

"Back to my shop. I'm going to stay there for a while. It's getting a little too crowded around here."

Bryce knew he was referring to Lucy being around so often. Had he been staying away because of it? "Clint, I want you to get to know Lucy. You'll see she's not what you think."

He shook his head. "You may trust her, Bryce, but I never will."

He walked out, and Bryce watched him get into his car and drive away.

He sighed, wishing his brother would give Lucy more of a chance to prove herself to him. She was doing everything in her power to establish Clint's innocence, and he didn't even seem to care.

He was heating a bowl of soup when Meghan arrived home from school. Her smile warmed his heart.

"Where's Lucy?"

"She's been working at the precinct today. They had a big break in the case."

"I like her, and I know you do too."

"Of course I like her."

"Are you going to marry her?"

He was so stunned by her question that he nearly

dropped his soup. "Why would you ask me something like that?"

She gave him a knowing stare that seemed to transcend her age. "You're scared, aren't you?"

"Of what?"

"Of being in love." She opened the drawer and handed him a spoon for his soup. "It's like when I first got Charlie. I didn't know him, but I wanted to believe in him. I wanted to believe he would hold me up and not let me down. I had to trust that he would do it, that he would take care of me. Now I know he will, but if I'd never trusted him, I wouldn't have known that. I would have lived my life too afraid to take that risk. I see you doing that. You like Lucy. I know you do. And she feels the same way. Why won't you take the risk?"

How could he explain to a thirteen-year-old girl that he was afraid of being heartbroken? Wouldn't that shatter her image of him. And when did she get so smart anyway? "I just—I just don't know, Meghan. You're right. I'm scared." He breathed in a heavy breath at the realization that he'd been trying so hard to hold back his feelings for Lucy.

Meghan put her arms around him and pulled him into a hug. "It's okay to be scared, Dad. I'm scared too. But how will you ever know if it can work if you don't take the risk?"

He hugged her back. "You're too smart for your own good, aren't you?"

"I miss my mom, but that doesn't mean I don't want someone in my life who can be that for me."

"I thought Cassidy could be that person for you. You two are close."

"I love Cassidy, but she doesn't fit. You know it. I know it. Even she knows it, though she might not want to admit it."

He watched his daughter leave the room and disappear into her bedroom. Her words floored him. Was it time to take that leap of faith with Lucy and tell her how he felt? His heart longed to be with her, but his mind kept racing, recalling all the times he'd been hurt when things were going well.

He shook off that regret. He couldn't change the past. He could only concentrate on the future, and he wanted to take that leap of faith with Lucy. He was ready.

They were so close to cracking this case. She could feel it. This guy was getting agitated and stressed out, and that could only be good for them. He was bound to make mistakes he wouldn't ordinarily make. Or else someone in town would notice his odd behavior and report him. Whichever the case, she could see his crime spree soon coming to an end.

And with that, her time in town would also come to an end.

Normally, she would be relieved to wrap up a case and get back to her apartment in Virginia, but there was no longer anything waiting there for her and nothing to draw her back. And everything in Whitten to stay for.

Her heart fluttered at the idea of remaining here, remaining with Bryce and Meghan and building a life. She hardly dared allow herself to even imagine it. She knew her feelings for Bryce had taken over control of her heart. But how would he feel about her when he discovered her involvement in killing a family?

She realized her mind was spiraling. She was stuck in a loop of imagining a future with Bryce while also imagining the disgust on his face when he knew the truth about Danny's wreck.

That's enough!

She couldn't deny her feelings any longer. She was falling in love with Bryce Tippitt. She wanted a future with him, but she couldn't even think about that anymore until she told him the real story about Danny and her own failure. It was time to come clean and let the chips fall where they may.

And there was no time like the present. She picked up her cell phone and dialed, unable to stop the lift of her heart when she heard his voice.

"Any leads from the press conference?" he asked.

They'd had several people call into the tip line after the press conference, but so far, the tips hadn't led anywhere. "We're still taking calls and sorting through evidence, but nothing so far."

"Something will break soon. Are you nearly finished there? I'm heating up some canned soup. It's not much, but Meghan seemed to tolerate it."

All she wanted in life besides capturing this killer was to fall into Bryce's arms and build a future with him, but before she would even allow herself to plan for that, she had to tell him the truth.

"There's something I need to tell you." She took a deep breath and blurted out the truth. "It's about Danny." No turning back now. He would be sure to ask her about him now that she'd brought it up. Would he feel she'd betrayed his friend by not noticing his drug addiction?

"You don't have to tell me," he said instead. "I know. I looked up news reports about the wreck the night we met."

She sucked in a surprised breath. He'd known all along and never said anything. "You knew?"

His voice softened. "I did. And Lucy, what happened wasn't your fault."

"I'm an FBI-trained profiler and I had no idea my fiancé was a drug addict. How can that not be my fault?" The ridiculousness of even hearing it said aloud struck her. Of course it was her fault.

"I'm sure he did his best to hide that from you."

"Four people died, Bryce. Four innocent people. The kids were only eight and ten. They didn't even have the opportunity to grow up and have a life before theirs were snuffed out due to Danny's selfishness." Tears ran down her face at the horror of it all. She flicked them away before she melted into a sobbing mess on the phone. At least he couldn't see her this way. "I've been questioning myself ever since. How can I be trusted to do my job, to read people and create accurate profiles of them, if I couldn't even tell my own fiancé was an addict?"

"You're human. No one can fault you for that. Besides, you weren't looking for profile information on the man you loved."

She was shocked by his lack of condemnation. "D-does that mean you don't hate me?"

"Hate you? Is that what you've been worried about? Oh, Lucy, you didn't ask for this to happen to you. You may feel guilt for your inability to stop it, but Danny was the one who chose to get into the car that day. He was the one who hid his problem from you. He might not have even realized he had a problem yet. Do I blame you? Of course not. Anyone who does is crazy. You're the most kind, loving person I've ever met." His words were like a balm to her bleeding heart, and she wished now she'd done this in person just so she could sink into his arms.

"I've been so afraid to tell you," she said. "This whole thing with Danny has affected everything. I haven't even been able to do my job properly because I'm so afraid everything I do is wrong. How can I trust my own judgment if I couldn't see that?"

"We all do the best we can for those we love," he told her. "It's all we can do. That and trust in God. Romans 8:1 says there's no condemnation in Christ Jesus. He's forgiven everything we've done or will ever do."

She knew the verse well and had repeated it often, but now it seemed much too simple for her situation. "I don't deserve forgiveness." Not from the Williams family, not from Bryce and certainly not from God.

"Too bad. It's been given. Maybe instead of spending time with me this evening, you should spend some time in the Word."

"I might do that," she told him, even though she was certain if she even tried to pick up a Bible, something terrible would happen. She knew her fears were irrational, but that didn't stop them from being real or from her feeling them.

"Don't let the fear win, Lucy. Too much is at stake. I had something I wanted to tell you too, but I don't think you're ready to hear it yet. Pick up the Word and dive into it. You'll find what you need to let go there, I promise. And whenever you're ready to talk more about it, I'll be around."

Tears rolled down her face at Bryce's comforting words. She was thankful for them.

She held on to the line even after he'd disconnected. She wanted to believe he was right, that God had already forgiven her. But what about the family of the people who'd died? What about Danny's family, who continued to blame her for not helping him? What about her own anger and resentments?

How could any of that ever be forgiven?

She was still holding on to the phone when Detective Ross entered the conference room. His face was pale and his countenance serious.

Lucy stood to face him, wiping away her tears before he could ask about them. "What's the matter? Has something happened?"

His voice was low and as serious as his expression. "I'll say it has. We received an email with the preliminary DNA results from the skin samples beneath your fingernails."

This was it. This was finally the moment this case would be settled once and for all. "Was there a match?"

He nodded. "They matched Clint Tippitt's. He is the Back Roads Killer."

Lucy dropped her cell phone, then reached to pick it up as the full force of what she'd just learned hit her. Clint had been the man who'd abducted her and murdered those women.

And her profile was completely wrong.

Bryce's arm was growing stiff from sitting around the house doing nothing. He was tired of being on the sidelines and was ready to get back to helping Lucy.

Their phone call earlier had changed things between them for the better. He could see a future with her now, and lots of brothers and sisters for Meghan.

He heard Meghan blow by him in a rush to change into her riding clothes. "I want to get Charlie a workout before it gets dark," she told Bryce, and he didn't argue. She loved being on that horse, and he was glad she had something in her life she was passionate about.

Clint wasn't far behind her, but Bryce was surprised to see him. He hadn't liked the way his brother had stormed off earlier, and Clint wouldn't like it when he discovered that Bryce hadn't taken his advice to stay away from Lucy.

But first, she needed to work through her guilt over Danny's death. That was something he could wish away for her, but he didn't have the ability to erase it.

Clint looked calmer now and even a bit apologetic as he sat at the table across from Bryce. "I'm sorry about earlier. I owe you an apology. You're entitled to date anyone you want to."

"Thanks. I appreciate that."

"In fact, I hope you're right about Lucy. I want to believe she's here to help me."

"She is. I didn't get a chance to tell you, but she doesn't believe you killed those women, Clint. She thinks the killer is older, like Mom and Dad's age. She thinks Amanda Lake, the woman Dad was accused of killing, was this killer's first victim."

"She's cleared Dad?"

He nodded, seeing Clint was coming over to his side where Lucy was concerned. "She said it's the same killer."

"But there's still the matter of Jessica."

Bryce leaned against the table and sighed. "I know. That doesn't clear your name on her case."

He reached into his pocket and pulled out a necklace, showing it to Bryce. "I found this. It belonged to Jessica."

"Where did you get this?"

"I've racked my brain ever since that night Jessica vanished for what could have happened to her. The only thing that makes sense is that she accidently drove into Lake Klein and drowned. It was on her way home, and it explains why she never made it."

"Didn't they search the lake?"

"Yes, but nothing else makes sense to me. A few years ago, I took scuba lessons and I've been searching the lake myself section by section."

Bryce was stunned by his brother's commitment to finding Jessica. It proved he was as good a person as Bryce knew he was.

"Last year, I found this necklace. It's Jessica's. I know it is. She was wearing it the night she left here. It proves to me she has to be in that lake."

Bryce stared at the necklace. If it was Jessica's, his brother was right. She must have gotten disoriented and driven her car into the lake that night. "Did you show this to the police?"

"No. They wouldn't believe me. But I thought maybe…" He took a deep breath then let it out, and Bryce could see he was worried but determined. "I thought Lucy might believe me and do something to help."

Bryce was certain she would do anything she could

to help Clint, but the most important thing was that his brother didn't feel so alone anymore. That was a good step in the right direction for reclaiming his life. "I'm sure she'll be glad to help. I'll ask her."

The sound of a car pulling into the yard grabbed his attention, and he walked to the door. Two police cruisers pulled into the driveway, followed by an SUV and an unmarked car.

Bryce's gut clenched as he stepped outside to face them. This could not be good.

Chief Dobson exited the SUV and approached the porch where Bryce stood with Clint.

"What's going on, Chief?" He spotted Lucy getting out of the unmarked car along with Detective Ross. "Lucy? What's happening?"

She walked around the front of the vehicle but kept her distance. "The DNA results came back," she told him. "They match Clint."

Bryce was stunned by her words. He turned to his brother, whose eyes widened in surprise.

"It's not true," Clint told him. "I didn't do anything." That old anger and cynicism he'd thought was gone had returned to his brother's face.

Chief Dobson held up a piece of paper. "Clint Tippitt, we have a warrant for your arrest in the abduction and attempted murder of FBI Agent Lucy Sanderson." He turned to the officers standing with him. "Take him into custody. For good this time."

Bryce jumped from the porch. "This is a mistake."

"Move out of the way, Bryce, or we'll take you in too."

The officers moved past him and handcuffed Clint

before leading him off the porch and into the back of one of the patrol cars. Before they pushed him inside, Clint looked back at him, his eyes pleading with Bryce to believe him, to believe in him.

"This is a mistake," Bryce insisted, but no one was listening.

The police had finally found the evidence they needed to arrest his brother, but the only thing that made sense to him was that this was all a terrible mistake.

"I'll ride back with the officers," Ross told Lucy before tossing her the keys to his car.

As the cruisers and the chief's SUV pulled away with Clint, Bryce turned and saw his daughter watching from the doorway. She looked as stunned and concerned as he felt. He wanted to offer her some words of assurance, but none would come.

His legs threatened to give out, so he sat down on the porch to try to get his bearings. This couldn't be happening. It just couldn't. He couldn't even process this. He didn't know where to turn or what to do to help Clint now.

His gut churned with a sad truth that right and wrong, truth and justice weren't always the same thing. The law said Clint was innocent until proven guilty, but his brother had been tried and convicted in this town a long time ago.

He glanced up and saw Lucy approaching. She appeared hesitant and cautious as she took a spot on the step beside him and reached for his hand. Her touch was like a balm against his bleeding heart, and he was thankful for it. He'd hoped with her arrival in town, the truth would finally clear his brother of the cloud that had loomed over him, and their family, for years, but it hadn't.

"Bryce, I'm sorry. I received the news not long after speaking with you earlier."

"He didn't do it. He didn't abduct you."

"He did, Bryce, and it's about time you face the truth. The lab report came back showing he was the person I scratched that night."

"Who has ever heard of getting DNA results back that quickly?"

"They were only preliminary results, but the FBI lab is reliable. It was him, Bryce. It's time you face that. This town is safer now that he's in custody, and so is your daughter. I'm sorry it had to turn out this way, but I don't create the bad guys. I only find them."

Suddenly her hand in his felt less like a balm and more like alcohol digging into an open wound.

"I know you want to help your brother, but you also have a daughter to think of too. I don't want to see you make a mistake and trust the wrong people."

He pulled his hand away as the realization that everything Clint had said about her was coming true. "No, this is a mistake. Your profile said—"

"My profile was wrong, Bryce. Don't you get it? I'm a fraud." She jumped to her feet. "Obviously, I have no idea what I'm doing as a profiler. DNA doesn't lie. Your brother abducted me and murdered those women."

He leaped to his feet. "That's not true!"

"It is true! And it's about time you realized it and moved on with your life. Your brother is a killer."

"Stop it! Stop it, both of you!" Meghan cried, jumping between them. "We have to stick together. We're a family, and that's what families do."

Bryce took her arm and pulled her out of the way, all his anger and frustration bent on lashing out at Lucy. "She's not family, Meghan. She's an impostor and a fraud."

He turned and stormed into the house, slamming the door. He had things to do, and he couldn't worry about Lucy or her feelings. He had to find a lawyer for his brother.

Lucy stood dumbfounded, staring at the front door. That had gone downhill fast, but what had she expected? She'd promised to clear his brother's name, but DNA evidence didn't lie.

Meghan grabbed her hand. "Lucy, please don't go."

She pulled her hand away. "I don't think your dad wants me here right now, sweetie. I should go." She turned and stumbled toward the car, but tears threatened her and she needed a moment to compose herself before she got inside.

She shouldn't have tried telling Bryce what was best for him and his daughter. They were none of her business, yet she felt a loss of something that might have been. She would have liked to pursue her feelings for Bryce to see if they could turn into something, but now she was certain that wasn't possible. She'd allowed her own emotions to color her judgment, as Bryce had. He couldn't see it, and he would never forgive her for putting his brother away. She didn't blame him for his brother's actions, but she couldn't ignore them either.

She pulled herself together long enough to get into

the car and drive away, but she doubted she would make it back to her hotel or the precinct before the tears came hot and angry. The sooner she was away from this town and Bryce Tippitt, the easier her life would be.

Who was she fooling? It would take her a long time to recover from Bryce Tippitt.

"Lucy."

She screamed and swerved when someone spoke her name. Tears clouded her vision, but in the rearview mirror she spotted Meghan pop up from the back seat.

"What are you doing here?" she demanded. She didn't plan on the angry tone of her voice, but not only had Meghan startled her, she'd also caught her at a very vulnerable moment. Lucy pulled the car to the side of the road.

"I wanted to talk to you."

"You didn't have to hide in my car to do so."

"After the scene between you and my dad back at the house, I doubted you would want to talk to me."

Meghan didn't deserve to be pulled into the middle of this, yet she had been, and Lucy felt ashamed at how she'd pulled away from the girl back at the ranch. "Get up here," she said, tossing her bag into the back seat. "You don't have to worry about talking to me, Meghan. I'm not so certain your dad would approve though."

"I know. That's why I hid. He shouldn't have spoken to you like that."

"Meghan, I appreciate the sentiment, but this is a very complicated matter."

"I don't like it when you fight. You and my dad are good together. I know he loves you, Lucy. Don't you love him?"

Her heart broke at the hope in the girl's eyes. She was just too young to understand all this. "It's not that I don't—"

"Do you love my dad, yes or no?"

"Of course I do," Lucy admitted. She loved him too much. That was the problem.

"Then why don't you make up and be together? I don't understand why you can't say you're sorry."

"It's not that simple," she said, already planning where she would turn around to drive Meghan back to the house.

Meghan was about to jump into the front seat when something crashed through the windshield. Meghan screamed from the back seat, and something grazed Lucy's arm.

Someone was shooting at them!

Lucy jammed the car back into drive and floored the accelerator, but not before another bullet pierced the car and hit her in the shoulder. Pain blinded her, and she lost control and ran off the road, smashing the car into a tree. Her head slammed against the airbag as it deployed and her vision blurred. She felt warmth flowing over her. It had to be blood. But she couldn't worry about herself.

"Meghan, are you all right?"

The girl moaned in pain, but her voice was a joyous sound when she responded from the back seat with, "I'm okay."

"Are you hurt?"

"I jammed my arm against the door. It hurts, but I'll be okay." She heard Meghan gasp. "Someone was shooting at us."

Lucy tried to move her arm to reach for the gun at her side. Pain riddled through her. She couldn't reach it. "Meghan, do you see anyone coming?"

She jerked around, glancing outside. "I don't see anyone. Do you think whoever shot at us is still out there?"

"We have to assume they are. Can you reach for my gun in my holster?"

Meghan leaned over the seat and grabbed it, gasping at the blood flowing down Lucy's arm. Before Lucy could take it, she spotted movement in her peripheral vision. She spun around as something heavy slammed against her head. She slumped over the steering wheel, and everything seemed to happen in slow motion after that as a figure appeared at the door.

"What are you doing?" Meghan screamed. "Why are you doing this?"

Lord, no! Please don't let him hurt Meghan.

The girl's voice grew muffled as darkness threatened to pull Lucy away. She wouldn't be able to help Meghan or herself. They were at the mercy of whoever had fired at them.

EIGHT

Her head was pounding as she awoke but her shoulders ached too, and it had everything to do with the hard concrete floor she was lying on. Lucy opened her eyes and saw a frightened and timid Meghan huddled in the corner, plastic zip ties around her hands.

Lucy jerked awake at that image, the memories of being ambushed rushing back to her. Her head protested, but she ignored the pain and sat up anyway, putting weight on her arm, an act that caused another shot of pain to rush through her—a reminder that she'd been shot. Her shoulder now had a freshly dressed bandage covering that wound. "Meghan, are you all right?"

Tears slid down the girl's cheeks, but she nodded. "I'm better now that you're awake. I was worried she'd killed you."

She?

"She who? Who did this?" Lucy glanced around. They were in what looked like the basement of a house. But whose house? And where were they? Her hands were bound too, but she tried to stand, her head again protesting, but she wanted a look out of the window high on the far wall. It was too narrow for her to crawl through, but she could at least get an idea where they were being held.

Lucy glanced through the window, and disappointment overwhelmed her. All she saw were trees and bushes. No houses were visible, and only a lone car sat outside. They were essentially out in the middle of nowhere. That wasn't good for them.

She turned back to Meghan, who was sobbing softly. "It's going to be okay, Megs. I'm going to get us out of this." She knelt beside her and touched her hands. "The woman who took us—did you recognize her?"

Meghan's eyes grew wide with fear and tears pooled in them, but she managed to nod.

"Who was it? Who did this?"

Meghan sniffed back more tears, then opened her mouth to answer. She slammed it shut when a shadow appeared on the stairs. Lucy turned, wishing she had a weapon of some kind, even a stick or a shovel to fight back with, but there was nothing within reach. It wasn't right that Meghan had been dragged into this too, and Lucy was determined to do everything in her power to make sure she was unharmed despite having her hands bound.

She leaned in front of Meghan to protect her as Lucy turned to face her abductor coming down the stairs.

Cassidy!

Lucy stood. "What's happening? Why are we here?"

"I brought you here. I dressed your wound too. I'm a nurse, remember."

"But why did you attack us, and why are you keeping us here?"

Cassidy's stare was ice-cold and emotionless as she gazed at Lucy, folding her arms. "You know why."

An understanding settled inside Lucy. She hadn't been imaging the possessive vibe she'd felt with Cassidy before, not by a long shot. "This is about jealousy?" It was so ridiculous that Lucy nearly laughed out loud, but stopped when she registered Cassidy's dead-serious demeanor.

The woman moved to the bottom of the staircase and stared down Lucy. "You think you can come to town and take Bryce away from me? Well, you're wrong. He's mine, and he'll always be mine. Do you think you're the first woman who's tried to take him from me? You're not."

"Cassidy, calm down. I'm not a threat to you. If you'll let us go, I'll leave town."

"Too late! I gave you opportunities to leave town, remember? Plenty of them. But you wouldn't leave. Now I'll make certain you never do."

So Cassidy had been behind the attacks against her the whole time, and each threat and attempt on her life had had nothing to do with the Back Roads Killer. More and more, her skills as a profiler were becoming laughable.

"I know you're angry with me, Cassidy, and you have every right to be, but what about Meghan? I know you don't want to hurt her."

Cassidy stared past her to Meghan, still sniffling in the corner. "Of course I don't want to hurt her." She moved toward Meghan in the corner and knelt in front of her. "But she's left me no choice." She stopped addressing Lucy and turned to Meghan. "You weren't supposed to be there," Cassidy told her. "You were supposed to be at home safe and sound. What were you doing with her?"

Lucy could see Cassidy was losing it. Was she angrier that Meghan was in danger, or that the girl had chosen to go somewhere with Lucy instead of with her? Lucy suspected it was the latter.

"I—I wanted to spend some time with her," Meghan said. Fear was flowing off her, and tears ran down her cheeks. "I-I'm sorry."

Cassidy rubbed her eyes, then stood up and paced. "It's going to be okay," she told Meghan, and Lucy was sure she meant it. She hadn't wanted to involve Meghan in this nightmare, but she had, and now Lucy knew she had to find a way out of it. Cassidy knelt beside Meghan again, and Lucy saw her face morph into the kind, caring woman Meghan knew. "It's going to be okay, honey. Nothing bad is going to happen to you. We'll go back to our normal lives, and everything will be okay. You want to see your dad again, don't you?"

Meghan sniffed, then nodded.

"Good. We'll just get in the car and go, and no one needs to know what happened here. We can say we decided to go into town for a girls' spa day. What do you think? He'll believe that, won't he?"

Meghan nodded, and Lucy could see she was beginning to believe the web of lies Cassidy was spinning.

"Good, good." Cassidy blew out a breath. "We'll be fine."

Meghan glanced over at Lucy, and Lucy nodded at her, trying to silently encourage her to go with Cassidy. She believed Cassidy truly didn't want anything bad to happen to her.

But Meghan wasn't going to understand that.

"What—what about Lucy?" she asked.

"She'll be fine," Cassidy said.

"C-can't she come with us?"

"No!" Cassidy knelt beside Meghan and tried to compose herself. "No. She's staying here. And we can't talk about what happened here, Megs. We can never speak about it. Do you understand? Bad things, terrible things, will happen if we do."

Lucy prayed the girl would stay quiet and accept the way out Cassidy was offering, but her hesitation spoke volumes. She was too much of a kind soul to leave Lucy behind.

"But—but, what about Lucy?"

Cassidy leaped to her feet and screamed at the girl. "Who cares about Lucy! I am so sick of hearing about Lucy. It's all you and your father ever talk about these days." She walked to the stairs and stomped up them, slamming the door at the top and locking it.

"I'm sorry," Meghan said, starting to cry again. She'd surely never seen Cassidy like this, and it frightened her. It frightened Lucy too, but she couldn't dwell on her fear. Cassidy had hinted that she'd killed other women who'd gotten in her way, and she'd already tried to kill Lucy multiple times. This time, she wouldn't miss.

She rushed to Meghan and did her best to comfort the girl. They both needed their wits about them if they were going to get out of this.

Bryce spent the next few hours on the phone trying to find his brother a good lawyer. He was going to need one, and it would be expensive, as he was going to have to bring one in from out of town. He'd already spoken to several local attorneys who weren't too keen about taking on a case where DNA evidence proved his brother's guilt. Finally he managed to find someone willing to come in tomorrow to at least talk about the case.

Bryce leaned back in his chair as the reality of the situation hit him. He still couldn't believe, couldn't even process, that Clint could be a serial killer. It didn't make any sense to him at all. How had the DNA evidence come back to implicate him? He'd so been looking forward to having it exonerate his brother.

And he owed Lucy an apology. He should never have said those terrible things to her. She had been the only person to stand behind him, and he'd lashed out at her for her role in Clint's arrest.

Lord, when will this nightmare be over?

He sighed and stood up. He would apologize to Lucy tomorrow, but for tonight, he had his family to think about. Meghan had been upset to see him and Lucy arguing. He needed to make things right with her.

He walked to the foot of the stairs and called up. "Meghan! Can you come down here please?" When she didn't respond, he figured she had on her headphones and couldn't hear him. He ascended the stairs and knocked on her door, then pushed it open when she didn't answer. She wasn't there.

He glanced out the bedroom window but didn't see her. He recalled her saying earlier she was taking Charlie out for a ride, but when he reached the barn, Charlie was there, still saddled and ready to ride. And Meghan was nowhere in sight.

He took out his phone and dialed her number, but

the call went straight to voice mail. "Meghan, call me when you get this."

He went back inside and searched the house for her, but she wasn't there. Mild panic was beginning to rise in him. She'd definitely been here when Clint was arrested and he and Lucy had fallen out, but Bryce couldn't recall seeing her after that. He'd been too preoccupied with his own anger and grief that he hadn't made certain his daughter was okay.

He dialed Lucy's number, hoping she recalled seeing where Meghan had gone, but her phone went to voice mail too.

Full-blown panic set in as the minutes ticked by without a return call. Meghan had been visibly upset. Maybe she'd called a friend to pick her up or started walking. He phoned her best friend, but she hadn't heard from Meghan either. She agreed to call around, but Bryce didn't wait for a return call. If Meghan hadn't called her friend and she wasn't on the property, she must have started walking. He could imagine a scenario where she was so angry with him that she would take a walk to cool off. But she should have been back by now... and a killer was still on the loose, regardless of what the police believed.

He hopped into his rented truck and took off down the driveway, but Meghan was nowhere in sight. He tried her phone again, then Lucy's. They both went straight to voice mail.

He rounded a curve and spotted a car rammed into a tree. His heart clenched when he recognized it as Ross's car. Lucy had been driving it when she'd left earlier.

Bryce pulled to the shoulder and hopped out. The

front end was damaged and the airbag had deployed, but it was the bullet hole in the window and the blood on the seat that grabbed his attention. The hole in the glass was too small to be from a tree branch. One that tiny wouldn't have had the power to break the glass. He recognized a bullet hole when he saw one, and the blood on the driver's seat told him Lucy had been hit by it. Someone had shot at her and run her off the road. He glanced around and called her name. But where was she?

A sound from the back seat spun him around. It was a cell phone, and he recognized the ring. He pushed open the door and found the phone on the back floorboards. He picked it up and confirmed his worst fear. It was his daughter's phone. There were multiple missed calls including two from him and one from her best friend moments ago. Meghan had been in this car when someone had shot at it.

His daughter and Lucy were both missing.

Lucy pulled at the binds on her hands as Cassidy sat on the steps several feet away from them, filling syringes with some sort of liquid. Meghan had finally cried herself to sleep, and Lucy was glad. She didn't want to frighten Meghan any more than she already was, but she could tell by Cassidy's demeanor that they were in real trouble. "What are those for, Cassidy? Are you going to use them on us? Is that your plan for getting rid of us?"

"It's not poison, if that's what you think. It's only a sedative, like the one I used to get you here after I knocked you out."

"Then what is your plan? What are you going to do to us?"

"I'm going to do what I wanted to do with the others, but it never worked out. It was much easier to mess with their brakes or burn down their house."

All the things she'd tried with Lucy. She felt her heart clench, recalling Bryce telling her how Meghan's mother had died in a car crash. Had Cassidy been behind that too? She was glad Meghan was sleeping so she wouldn't overhear this conversation. "Did you—did you kill Meghan's mother?"

Cassidy stopped and looked at her, her eyes cold and hard before she turned back to her work. "She was becoming a problem. Besides, I thought once she was gone, me and Bryce and Meghan would be one big happy family. That didn't work out."

Dread filled her, and not just because Meghan had lost someone she cared about, but because it meant Cassidy had killed before—and their chance for survival had just grown even more bleak. She wouldn't hesitate to kill them, not when she'd done it at least once before.

"You said *them*. Plural. Have there been others?"

"A few. There was a woman at the diner who smiled one too many times at Bryce. She thought it was funny when I told her he was mine. She didn't think it was too funny when her car sank to the bottom of the lake, especially since she was in it at the time. And a few others who tried to get too close to him."

Her mind went to one woman who had never been accounted for. "What about Jessica? Did you kill Jessica too?"

Cassidy gave her a confused look. "Why would I hurt Jessica? She barely knew Bryce. She only had eyes for his brother. I never touched her."

Lucy was stunned by the warped logic of her words. She wanted to scream at her to try to knock some sense into her. "How can you do this? I know Bryce never asked you to do this."

"He didn't have to ask me. I understand how important it is to take care of these things. I cannot allow anyone to get in the way of our relationship."

"Even Meghan? Think about Bryce and what he'll do without Meghan."

"I never wanted to hurt her," Cassidy said. "But she chose you over me, and I can't allow that. It'll hurt him, but I'll be there to offer him comfort. We'll get past this tragedy together."

Lucy's mind grappled with something she could do or say to reach Cassidy, to change her mind. She thought about what Bryce had said about Cassidy's difficult childhood and her parents moving around so often. Perhaps something in their constant moves had given the woman such terrible abandonment issues that she could no longer distinguish right from wrong.

She opened her mouth to speak but zeroed in on the syringes instead, and something in her brain clicked as all the pieces fell into place: the FBI report that showed murdered women matching the killer's MO all over the country. The Summers family's constant moves. The syringe the Back Roads Killer had tried to inject her with the night he'd abducted her. The inconsistencies in Paul Summers's story.

And suddenly Lucy realized Cassidy's childhood had been much more difficult than any of them realized.

"How long have you known your dad was a serial killer?" She'd finally put it all together. Paul Summers had killed Amanda Lake and allowed his friend to take the blame for it. His wife's job had taken them all over the country, but when she'd retired, they'd moved back to Whitten months before the killings started up again.

Cassidy snorted and gave her a look that seemed to say, *so what, you figured it out.* "Too long."

"And you never told anyone?"

"I did once. I told my mom that I suspected Daddy had done something terrible. She slapped me and told me to keep my mouth shut. She told me we had to keep the secret or else our family would be destroyed."

"You were a kid then. Why have you never told anyone now, even after these women went missing?"

"Are you crazy? Do you think I want to be known as the daughter of a serial killer? Do you think anyone would ever want me after that? Do you think Bryce would have anything to do with me, knowing that I helped frame his brother for the things my own father did?"

"He might be grateful you cleared his brother's name."

"No, he would never forgive me. I cannot be the girl whose dad is a killer. I lived with that fear all my life, wondering and believing that everyone knew something was wrong with my family. My mother constantly told me we had to keep the secret. That we couldn't let anyone tear our family apart."

Part of Lucy was saddened to think of how Cassidy grew up. It must have been a very difficult childhood. "I'm sorry," she said, and she meant it. No child should grow up with such knowledge. It would have been better for her to be ignorant of her father's deeds.

"I just wanted to get away from him, away from the knowledge of what he'd done. That's why I moved back here in high school. I was terrified of what he might do. I begged my mother to let me come. She wouldn't leave him. I never understood why she stayed, but now I think she was as afraid of the scandal as I am now. But then when she retired and they moved back here, I knew it was only a matter of time before he would start again."

"And you gave him the drugs he uses to sedate his victims?"

"No. My mother used to be a pharmaceutical rep. I'm pretty sure he stole the drugs from her. But when she retired a few months after they'd moved back, I caught him stealing from the supply cabinet at the hospital. He didn't know I'd seen him. When he was gone, I covered up what he'd done. It was easier than I thought it would be. Security procedures in that hospital aren't very up-to-date."

"Cassidy, you have the opportunity to be the hero here. You can turn him in. It'll make the news, sure, but you'll be the hero. The woman who turned in a serial killer."

"I don't want that kind of notoriety. I only want to be left alone. Can't you understand that? You came here to destroy us, to destroy everything I've built here."

"I didn't do that, Cassidy. Your father did that."

She shook her head. "I never wanted this. I only wanted you to leave."

"You know I couldn't do that." Lucy saw the regret in her face and sucked in a breath. "What are you going to do to us?"

She turned and looked at Lucy. "I told you. What I wanted to do with the others but couldn't. I'm giving you to him."

"What do you mean you're giving us to him?" It didn't make sense. Would a killer really take an offering from his daughter?

"You're wondering if he knows I know his secret. I'm sure he does, but it's not something we ever talk about. I could never leave you on the doorstep for him. That wouldn't do. He's a hunter, you know. He lives for the hunt. I'll have to leave you where he can find you. I've become quite good at figuring out when he's going out hunting and where he'll be. I can tell when he's in his killing mood."

Lucy knew they were in trouble as Cassidy slipped the syringes into her pocket and walked out. She heard doors closing, then the start of an engine. Cassidy was leaving, probably going to set up her plan to hand them over to be tortured and murdered at the hands of a serial killer. She'd already justified her actions, and she'd had many years, apparently, to come to grips with what she'd done.

She glanced over at Meghan. She had to do something, anything, to get them out of this. This was no longer just about saving herself. She couldn't allow this young girl to pay for the sins of others because she hadn't seen or noticed that Cassidy was a psychopath. She pulled at the binds again, grimacing as the zip tie dug into her wrists. She had to find something to cut them off. She would never pull herself free of them.

She should have seen this happening. This was Danny all over again. No, she wasn't close enough to Cassidy to relate this to Danny. She should have seen the truth about Danny, but she'd spent enough time with Cassidy that something should have at least tickled her senses. She was a trained profiler and she'd allowed yet another offender to fly under her radar, and now her life and a young innocent girl's were on the line.

She scooted over to a rusty nail on the wall. It was behind her and several inches higher than she was, so it was awkward to get in position to rub it against her binds. Her shoulder cried out at the action, but she crawled up onto her knees, lifted her arms and was able to reach it. Hopefully, she could get free before Cassidy returned. She had no idea how the woman planned to deliver her and Meghan to her father, but the idea was terrifying. She would have to incapacitate them in some way to keep them from escaping the way Lucy had previously. That was probably what the syringes were for. Meghan was too young for such trauma.

God, are You there? Are You listening? We need You to intervene.

Why was she praying? Would God even hear her? Or had she messed up too many times for Him to listen? She owed a life for the deaths of the family Danny killed. She bore the responsibility and would gladly pay the price if that's what it took, but Meghan didn't deserve to die. She didn't have a debt on her shoulders.

Lucy fell as her strength gave out. She tugged at the binds and realized the nail wasn't cutting through. Her bandage darkened as her wound started bleeding again. Tears rolled down her face. She was so tired, and time was running out.

NINE

For once, the police sirens were music to his ears. Detective Ross hopped out of a patrol car as it rolled to a stop near where his car was smashed into a tree.

"What happened?"

"I came upon it like this. There's a bullet hole in the window and blood on the seat." He pointed toward more drops on the ground. "There's some here too. It looks like Lucy made it out of the car, but the trail ends abruptly. My guess is whoever did this put her into another car."

Ross nodded and pulled out his cell phone. "I've got a team on the way."

Bryce also showed him Meghan's phone. "It was in the car too, in the back seat. She must have sneaked into the car before Lucy left."

Ross tried to reassure him. "If she's with Lucy, then she'll be okay. She'll take care of her."

Yes, Bryce had to remember that. Lucy loved his daughter. They'd gotten extremely close since she'd come to town. She wouldn't let anything happen to Meghan if she could help it.

His daughter's life was in her hands, and he had no choice but to trust her with it.

* * *

Lucy rubbed at the zip ties again and again until finally, thankfully, they split. She pulled the binds from her wrists, tossed them aside and stood up. Meghan was still asleep, and Cassidy hadn't returned yet.

She hurried up the stairs, unsurprised to find the door locked. She kicked at it several times but it didn't budge. The door looked new and the lock secure.

Her kicking woke Meghan, who realized she was free. "How did you get loose?"

Lucy ran back to her and pried the rusty nail from the wall. She used it to cut Meghan free, angry when she saw the raw skin from the zip ties on Meghan's wrists. "We have to get out of here now before she returns."

"Where's Cassidy?"

"I don't know, but I'm sure she'll be back soon. We need to go now."

Meghan's chin quivered. "I heard what she said about her father. You thought I was asleep, but I heard it. She's going to give us to the killer, isn't she?"

Lucy grabbed the girl's shoulders. "I'm not going to let that happen. We're getting out of here now."

She helped Meghan to her feet and steadied the girl as she took her hand and led the way to the small window and found an old piece of wood in the corner to shatter the glass. Meghan screamed as it rained down, but Lucy was more concerned about getting through it. Meghan might have no problem, but Lucy was bigger and the opening was narrow.

She helped Meghan up onto her shoulders and the girl easily shimmied through, reaching back inside to help Lucy. She grabbed her hand and pulled herself up, pain ripping through her from the wound on her shoulder and hampering her strength to climb up the wall.

She sighed and dropped to her feet. She simply couldn't get up there, but she had to get Meghan to safety. No matter what happened to her, she couldn't allow the girl to suffer for adult problems. It wasn't her fault she was in this mess. She'd trusted Cassidy. They all had.

"You have to go," Lucy told her. "Run and get help. Hurry before Cassidy comes back."

But Lucy saw the same stubborn determination she saw in Bryce on the girl's face. "No, I won't leave you." She reached down again. "Grab my hand. I'll pull you up."

Lucy reached for her and was nearly through the window when a car pulled into the driveway. "It's her! Run, Meghan, run! Don't stop for anything."

"I won't leave you!" she cried.

"Meghan, you have to run. Get to the police. That's how you'll help me." She let go of Meghan's hand and fell back to the basement floor. "Now, go before she sees you."

Meghan scurried away. Lucy tried to watch her through the opening as she hid behind a tree while Cassidy got out of her car. But Meghan tripped over a branch and let out a cry that grabbed Cassidy's attention as she headed for the door. She dropped the bags in her hands and shouted for Meghan.

"Get back here!" she cried, reaching into her pocket for a gun and firing.

Lucy screamed but Meghan took off running, even as the firing continued.

"Keep going!" Lucy shouted to the girl through the window. "Run!"

Cassidy ran after her, but Meghan disappeared into the brush.

Lucy tried to pull herself up again to see what was happening. Neither woman was in sight, but she hadn't heard any more gunfire either. That was a good sign. After several minutes, she spotted Cassidy returning alone, anger settling on her hard face as she stomped toward the house and slammed the door.

A moment later the basement door opened, and Cassidy hurried down the steps. Lucy backed away, ready to fight, but that proved to be short-lived when Cassidy raised the gun at her.

Still, Lucy had to chuckle. "It's over, Cassidy. She's gone, and she's going to tell everyone what you've done. She's even going to tell Bryce how you tried to kill her."

"You did this!" Cassidy's nostrils flared and she lifted the gun again, but Lucy was no longer afraid of her. She couldn't hurt her now. Shooting her now would save her the torture of being handed over to the Back Roads Killer.

But Cassidy didn't fire it. Instead, she used the butt end to smack Lucy. Pain ripped through her, but it couldn't wipe away the relief she felt even when Cassidy injected something into her neck. A sedative, no doubt, like the one her father had used.

Meghan had escaped. She would be found and Bryce would soon be reunited with his daughter.

Please, God, protect her. Keep her safe.

It was her only thought as darkness pulled her away.

As night began to fall, Bryce was beside himself with worry. Where were his daughter and Lucy? He recalled the scene with the car and blood on the seat.

It hadn't been much, but someone was clearly hurt—probably Lucy, as she would have been driving. At least they hadn't found any bodies. But if they'd escaped the shooter, then where were they?

Ross approached him with an update. "The GPS on the car doesn't indicate it went anywhere else besides leaving your place. Whatever happened to them happened here. The real question is, did they run from whoever did this or were they taken?"

Bryce was sure of the answer to that question. "Lucy would have found a way to contact someone by now. They were taken."

"Well, I've got a team starting a search of the wooded area around the car just in case. And I'm calling in bloodhounds."

Ross's determination to find them should have given Bryce hope, but he feared the worst. And after the confrontation he'd had with Lucy, he hated to think that might be the last words he would ever say to her. It sickened him to think that. No, he couldn't believe it. He had to have another opportunity to apologize to her.

And Meghan. His heart wrenched again. What would he do if he lost her too? How would he go on? He couldn't even think about that.

His phone buzzed in his pocket and he pulled it out. He didn't recognize the number, but he answered it anyway. It might be someone with information.

His heart leaped into his throat when he heard his daughter's voice. "Daddy?"

"Meghan, where are you?"

Another voice came on the line. "Mr. Tippitt, this is Officer Daniels. Your daughter flagged me down from the side of the road. We're en route now back to the station."

"I'll meet you there," Bryce told the officer. He motioned toward Ross. "It's Meghan. They found her."

He jumped into Ross's borrowed vehicle and they headed back into town, his heart hammering. His daughter was safe, but the officer hadn't mentioned anything about Lucy. If Meghan was on her own, then what had happened to Lucy?

Ross's phone rang and he answered it, his face turning grim as he listened. "Get cars over there now." He ended the call and glanced at Bryce.

His worst fears rushed through him. Had they found Lucy dead? "Whatever it is, tell me."

"Meghan told Officer Daniels who abducted her. It was Cassidy Summers."

His words stunned Bryce to the core. Cassidy? It wasn't possible. She was his best friend. She wouldn't hurt Meghan or Lucy. There had to be some mistake. Meghan must have misunderstood the officer's questioning.

"We're sending cars to her house now," Ross said, and all Bryce could do was nod. He couldn't have heard him correctly. It didn't make any sense that Cassidy was behind this.

They reached the precinct first and Bryce paced, waiting until a car appeared. His heart flip-flopped when he spotted Meghan in the passenger's seat. The car stopped at the curb, and she swung open the door.

"Megs!" He rushed to her as she called to him. He closed the gap between them in seconds, and held her as she collapsed in his arms.

He forced himself to look at her, seeing dirt and cuts and bruises. But overall, she looked unharmed. She was wearing a jacket he didn't recognize, and was cold to the touch. "Meghan, what happened? Where have you been?"

"Oh, Daddy." She dug her face into his chest and sobbed.

He wanted to comfort her, but he needed answers too. "Meghan, are you hurt?"

"I'm okay. She saved me, Daddy."

"Who did, Megs? Who saved you?"

"Lucy. She risked her life to save me."

His emotions were all over the place at hearing those words. Gratitude that she'd helped his daughter. Fear about what had happened to her. "Where is Lucy now, Meghan?"

"We were locked in the basement. Lucy made me climb out the window, but she couldn't get through it. Daddy, we have to help her. She's in danger."

"Who has her, Meghan? Tell me who was holding you hostage." He was hoping, praying, for an answer different from the one Ross had given him, but it didn't come. Her young face held shock and fear as she looked up at him.

"It was Cassidy, Dad. Cassidy said she was going to kill us."

She dug into his chest again while Bryce struggled to regain himself. He didn't doubt the truth of her words, but he needed to know the entire story.

He walked Meghan inside and tried to warm her up. He took her into one of the interview rooms for privacy and pulled out a chair for her before fetching her a bottle of water. She drank from it and sighed with relief.

"Tell me what happened, Meghan. Why did you go with Lucy?"

"I only wanted to talk to her. I heard you both arguing, and I knew she was leaving. I wanted to ask her to give you a second chance."

"Why would you do that, Meghan? You sneaked into her car?"

"Because I like her, Dad, and I know you do too. I thought we would be a family, but you were messing it up."

He knew she was right. He had messed it all up and would give anything to make it up to Lucy, but first he had to find her.

"What happened then?"

"When she realized I was there, she was turning around to take me back home when someone started shooting at us. Lucy lost control and wrecked the car. I hit my head, but I woke up to find the window shattering and Cassidy pulling Lucy from the car. I couldn't help it. I was so scared, I started screaming. That's when Cassidy realized I was in the car." She took a sip from her water bottle before continuing, and Bryce noticed her hands were shaking from her ordeal. "She was shocked to see me, but then she got angry and said I liked Lucy more than her. She had a gun and she said she would kill us if we didn't come with her. I was terrified, but Lucy was calm. She told me it was going to be okay, and I believed her."

Anger surged through him that someone he cared

about, someone who had been his closest friend, could do this to his daughter and the woman he loved.

"Cassidy tied us up and hid us in the basement." Meghan's eyes widened. "Then she said she was going to hand us over to her father, and we would never be seen again."

"What did she mean when she said she was going to hand you over to her father?"

"I didn't know at first, but Lucy figured it out. Cassidy's father, he killed those women, Dad, the women Uncle Clint was accused of killing."

Paul Summers? A killer? His mind couldn't process it, but it was no more unlikely than Cassidy kidnapping Lucy and his daughter and threatening to make them disappear.

He glanced over Meghan's head to the two-way mirror and wondered if Ross had been watching and listening. He opened the door to the interview room a moment later and called Bryce outside.

He rubbed Meghan's shoulders. "I'll be right back." She gripped his hand, and he could see she was terrified. "It's okay. I'm only going to step outside to talk to Detective Ross. I won't be far."

He pushed open the door and saw Ross standing there waiting for him. "No one was home at the Summerses' house. I've put out a BOLO on Cassidy's car."

"Did you overhear what Meghan said about Cassidy's father?"

He nodded. "I did. It's unbelievable that this is happening. How could he have been right under our noses all this time? I've already got men out searching. I'll move them to scour the roads for signs of either Paul's or Cassidy's car."

"What about Mrs. Summers? Has anyone been in contact with her?"

"No, but we'll find something. At least now we know what we're looking for."

"I don't want to leave Meghan. I should take her to the hospital to get checked out."

"Okay. If she says anything else, text me. I'll have to get her official statement at some point. See if she can remember where she was being held."

"I'll try. She's pretty shaken up."

He walked back into the room to sit with his daughter. She was the only link they had now to finding Lucy. He prayed it wasn't too late.

He shuddered at the idea of Cassidy saying she would turn them over to her father. The implications of that statement were ridiculous. She had to have known her father was the one responsible for the deaths of all those women and had said nothing, even while Clint was being accused and having his name smeared. And while his own father was labeled a murderer.

"Meghan, we really need to find Lucy. Detective Ross spoke with the officer who picked you up. He found you wandering down Grants Way Road. How long had you been walking when he found you?"

"I don't remember. Maybe a half hour."

"What direction were you coming from? Do you know where Cassidy was keeping you?"

"It was an old cabin in the woods. I'd never seen it before, but it took me a while to reach the road so I know it was far off."

He looked up as the door opened slightly, and Ross nodded at him. He'd heard it all and would send officers to search that area.

"That's good, Meghan. You did great. Now let's get you to the hospital."

She nodded and did as he asked, and although he did his best to remain calm on the outside for her sake, inside he was reeling.

A hidden cabin in the woods. How would they ever find Lucy before it was too late?

Lucy awoke, realizing she was in the back seat of a car. Her ears were ringing and her head pounded. Then she remembered Cassidy injecting her with something. She pulled herself up. The car was parked on the side of the road, the flashers on and the hood up. She reached for the door handle and pulled it, but nothing happened.

"You didn't think it would be that easy, did you?"

She glanced up. Cassidy stood outside the partially lowered window, watching her.

"Child locks," she said, grinning. "They're supposed to keep small children from opening the door from the inside, but they work on adults too. Oh, and if you're thinking about crawling into the front to get out—" she held up a gun aimed directly at Lucy "—I wouldn't try it."

Lucy's mind scrambled to make sense of this amid the fog of whatever Cassidy had injected into her. "What's the plan here, Cassidy?"

"The plan is to leave you here. When he drives by and catches sight of you, no one will ever see you alive again."

The coldness in her tone sent shivers through Lucy. "How do you know he'll come? You couldn't have called him."

"I've lived with him long enough to know when he's hunting, and I've figured out his hunting routes. I followed him to this stretch of road. He'll see the car, think you've broken down and stop on the pretense to help, but when he sees you're alone, well...that will be the end of you once and for all."

She had to force herself to stand, to get away, but whatever Cassidy had injected her with was still fighting in her body. Her legs were like rocks, and she could barely lift herself from the seat. If Cassidy was right, if he came before she got her strength back, she was done for.

"But what about the car?" Her best bet was to keep Cassidy talking, and maybe she would be distracted and Lucy could find a way to escape. She willed her legs to work, but nothing happened.

"I stole it from a grocery store parking lot. The police will find it abandoned tomorrow morning and return it to the owner. They'll probably write it up as kids joyriding."

Headlights flashed over the vehicle. Lucy tensed, and she saw Cassidy's face change. "He's coming." She darted away. Lucy lifted herself enough to see her vanish into the wood line.

The headlights were now blinding as a car pulled to the side of the road. Lucy heard the slam of a door and the crunch of gravel beneath someone's feet as they approached the car.

He was coming!

She used her arms to try to lift herself to the window. She had to do something to escape, or she would die tonight and two killers would go free. Cassidy would succeed in fooling everyone. Unless Meghan had managed to escape and tell Bryce and the police what she'd done.

Crunch, crunch.

Crunch, crunch.

The footsteps moved closer. Lucy stared toward the lifted hood, watching and waiting for the man to come into sight. The doors were locked, and even if she could open them, she didn't have the strength to run.

She was trapped.

A silhouette against the headlights appeared at the front of the car. He bent down through the open window and leaned inside, seeing Lucy on the seat, unable to move. She must appear an easy prey, just as his daughter had planned.

He opened the front door and leaned inside. Lucy knew in that instant she was looking into the face of a killer.

TEN

In the glow of the headlights, she saw his face and was surprised when a pleasant smile spread across it as he motioned to her. "Having a bit of car trouble, are you, Agent?"

Lucy shrank from him as best she could, but her limbs were still unwilling to cooperate. She knew how she must look. Someone who'd drank too much or done too many drugs and crawled into the back seat to sleep it off.

When she didn't answer, he continued, in a surprisingly pleasant voice. "What seems to be the problem?"

She couldn't answer, couldn't respond. All she heard was the loud thumping of her own heart. His eyes roamed over her, taking it all in.

Then he stood and glanced around again before spinning on his heel and heading back to his car. "I'll phone the police for you. They can come get you and take you home." She heard his footsteps on the gravel, moving away from her, and a sigh of relief rushed through her.

For about ten seconds.

"You're leaving?" came the cry from the woods.

Lucy couldn't see what was going on, but she recognized Cassidy's voice. She was confronting her father for not taking Lucy.

Panic gripped Lucy. She had to escape from this car now. Cassidy's father had left the door open, and she gripped the seat and dragged herself toward it. She couldn't afford to be locked in this car again—who knew what would happen with Cassidy? Her father might not kill her, but Cassidy was in way too deep to walk away. Either way, she had to escape. If her legs wouldn't cooperate, then she would crawl.

The commotion continued between the cars. Lucy couldn't see them, but she heard their voices shouting.

"Cassidy, what are you doing here?"

"You didn't take her!" Cassidy's voice was shrill and hysterical. She was on edge, hollering at a serial killer.

"I don't know what you're talking about."

"I left her for you, and after all the terrible things you've done, when I need you to be what you are, you're bailing on me?"

"Cassidy."

"Don't touch me!" she shrieked.

Gravel dug into Lucy's hands as she slid from the car. If they were at the front, she would head for the back, using her arms and elbows to belly crawl away. Slowly, her feet were coming back to life and pitching in with the effort, but they were still too weak to hold her weight.

"What has gotten into you, Cassidy?"

"I have lived with the monster you are all my life, terrified of what you would do to me. Now, when I need you to be that monster, you're leaving. You take her, Dad, and you'd better kill her before she exposes us both."

Lucy heard a slap, and from beneath the car saw Cassidy hit the ground.

"Don't you ever speak to me like that," he growled. Lucy couldn't see his face, but she heard the monster in him let loose.

Lucy saw him kneel and grab Cassidy around the throat. She still couldn't see his face, but she saw Cassidy's, and it was full of panic and fear.

"I didn't take her because I thought I saw someone run into the woods. I felt the setup from the get-go, and I wasn't going to risk it. As for handing her to me, no one gives me anyone. I take them. I'm a shark, Cassidy, and we don't wait around to be fed. We smell the blood in the water and strike."

Cassidy flailed on the gravel. "Please, don't. I needed to get rid of her. She can expose us both."

"Then you should have killed her yourself. And you definitely should have kept your nose out of my business."

He pressed his hand into her neck, and Lucy saw Cassidy struggle. She wished for the gun at her hip or some sort of weapon to fight him off with, but she knew she couldn't. Whatever Cassidy had injected her with hadn't yet worn off completely.

Cassidy grabbed his hand and kicked and flailed for several minutes, but his hand was steady as she flailed about. Finally, Cassidy went limp and Lucy saw her head roll as he released his grip.

She was dead.

Paul Summers stood, and his footsteps headed her way toward the back of the car.

He'd murdered his own daughter. And now, he was coming for Lucy.

Two hours after she'd been found wandering, Meghan was hooked up to a drip at the hospital. The doctors had checked her over, and aside from being dehydrated and bruised, she appeared to be fine.

Bryce spotted Detective Ross in the hallway and walked out to see him, praying for good news. "We think we've found the cabin. I'm sending in a team."

"I want to be there," he stated, and Ross agreed. "Let me tell Meghan where I'm going."

"I'll post an officer at her door," Ross offered, and Bryce was glad of it. He hadn't told any of the nurses or hospital staff about Cassidy, but he knew the word had spread that Meghan had named her as her kidnapper. That gave him some relief, that she wouldn't dare try to show her face at the hospital.

He suited up with the other men and rode with Ross as they prepared to take the cabin. Bryce's stomach clenched as they approached it. It was in such an isolated place that it was a wonder they'd found it at all. He spotted the busted-out basement window. They were definitely in the right place.

"How did you find this?"

"The deed is in Arlena Summers's name. We tracked her down at a church dinner and questioned her. She mentioned that Cassidy sometimes liked to come here for peace and quiet."

He didn't care how they'd found it, only that they

had. Bryce took out his gun. Ross wouldn't allow him to be the first to enter, but he wanted to be inside that cabin.

The team motioned when they were ready, then burst through the door, guns raised and on alert. The cabin looked empty when Bryce stepped inside. There were no flames in the fireplace, but the ashes were still warm, indicating it hadn't been lit long ago.

"The cabin is clear," one officer told Ross.

He sighed as Bryce looked around. "We're too late. Where would they have gone?"

Bryce glanced out at the dark night sky, and the terrible truth hit him. "If Meghan's right and her plan is to hand Lucy over to her father, she went to meet him."

"Great. Now we need to know where he is."

Officer Jenkins burst through the door, his face red and anxious. "Sir, it just came over the radio. They found a woman on the side of the road off Lakeshore Road."

Bryce felt the air leave his lungs, and the words nearly toppled him. Ross nudged him along as they got into the car to head to that scene. He'd made certain to leave a team behind to process the cabin.

Lakeshore Road was only a few miles from their location, and they arrived to find two patrol cars already at the scene taping it off. Bryce got out and headed over. He had to know. He had to see for himself. His world was spinning, and he felt sick as he approached a car with the hood up.

"What happened?" Ross demanded.

"At first, we thought it was a car that had broken down, but then we found the body. It turned out the car was reported stolen."

Bryce stepped around toward the front of the car and spotted legs on the ground. He felt sick, wondering if his world was about to crumble.

"Do you have identification on the victim?"

"Nothing was on her, but several of the officers recognized her." The way they glanced at Bryce made him ill. He walked around the car and glanced at the body on the ground. "It's Cassidy Summers."

He let out a breath he'd been holding. Cassidy, not Lucy. He couldn't process that at the moment. Ross bent down and examined bruises on her neck.

"It looks like she's been strangled." He stood and glanced at the car.

"If Meghan's right her plan was to hand Lucy over to her father. The stolen car, the hood up like it was broken down—do you think she was trying to lure him here?"

"Why wouldn't she just give her to him?"

"Because she's not supposed to know he's a cold-blooded killer." He recalled Cassidy's uneasiness with her father. Something had always been off about their relationship, and Bryce had sometimes wondered if Cassidy was frightened of him. She'd learned early on to protect herself. Now he knew why. She'd been living with a monster most of her life. He had no idea at what point she'd figured out what her father had been doing, but there must have been clues that caused her unrest.

"She sometimes talked about her father's actions that caused her family grief. It was something about the way she said it, like it was a euphemism. Now I know it probably was. It's obvious she knew about his deeds, but maybe she was trying to give him Lucy without him knowing about it, and he caught her."

Ross sighed and turned back to the body on the ground. "So he killed his own daughter and abducted Lucy."

Bryce swallowed the lump in his throat. One of his worst fears was coming true, despite the respite he'd gotten at finding Meghan safe. Lucy was in the hands of a killer.

The trunk popped open and Lucy tried to jump out, but Paul Summers blocked her path.

"Not so fast," he commanded, grabbing her by her bound hands and yanking her from the trunk.

She tried again to jerk away from him, and he turned and backhanded her. "I said stop!" he bellowed.

Pain ripped through her face and the force knocked her to her knees, but Paul pulled her back up. The gun in his belt was a constant reminder that he was in charge, and she needn't bother trying to escape.

She glanced around, taking in her surroundings. The only way she was going to make it out of this alive was if she had some clue as to where she was. He'd driven for what seemed like an hour before pulling into this lot, and she saw he was dragging her into an old, abandoned factory. No other cars were around, and she couldn't hear a single sound. They were in the middle of no-where. He had effectively cut her off from civilization.

God, how am I going to get out of this?

Hopefully, Meghan had made it back to Bryce safely. Knowing that he wouldn't lose his daughter too was her only consolation.

He'd been right about Clint. She didn't understand it, but obviously Clint hadn't been the one to abduct her.

She'd trusted the evidence instead of her own instinct, and look where it had gotten her. She didn't understand that DNA result, but obviously it was wrong. Clint wasn't the killer she'd been hunting for. Paul Summers was.

Paul dragged her inside and to a back part of the old factory. There she saw shiny new chains mounted on the wall. He'd set up shop here after they'd discovered his kill shed. And Lucy would be the first to experience it.

He pulled her over and clamped the heavy chains onto her arms above her head. She grimaced at the pain ripping through her shoulder, but she wouldn't give him the satisfaction of seeing her suffer. She was trapped, and she was going to die here tonight.

He went back to the car, then returned with a case, which he made a show of placing in front of her and opening. Inside was another new purchase. Knives to replace the ones the police had confiscated. He'd restocked and was ready to get back to his killing ways. Even being raided by the police hadn't stopped his thirst for blood.

He took one out and held it, pressing the flat side against her cheek. It was cold but not nearly as cold as the emotionless void in his eyes. He gave her a smug smile.

"You and I are going to have some fun tonight, Lucy."

She had no hope of being rescued. Even if Meghan had found help—and Lucy hoped she had—they had no way to find her. She was trapped out here with a madman intent on fulfilling his murderous desires, and no one was coming to rescue her.

Yet she deserved this after the way she'd failed to recognize Danny's drug problem. Didn't she?

Bryce's words returned to her. Jesus had already paid that price. Any failure on her part had long ago been forgiven and tossed into the deepest depths of the ocean. She didn't have to pay the price again. She'd been forgiven! And she wanted to live.

Lord, I don't want to die here!

But she would unless God intervened.

Tears rolled down her face. She couldn't wipe them away, but she wouldn't have even if she could. All her hopes and dreams of a future with Bryce, of building a life with him and Meghan, were never going to happen. She had no illusions of being rescued. Hopefully, Bryce and the police were focused on finding and rescuing Meghan. But if dying was the price she had to pay to keep Meghan safe, she would do it, and it had nothing to do with her needing redemption or making up for her failure with Danny. She didn't need that anymore. She understood now that those things had been forgiven long ago.

As she closed her eyes and accepted her fate, her only thoughts were of Bryce and Meghan, and how much she wished she could have been a more permanent part of their lives.

Bryce had to do something besides sitting around the precinct waiting for news from Ross. He was trying his best to get a warrant for Paul Summers's GPS coordinates, but it was slow coming. Bryce could have gone to the hospital, but he hadn't wanted to worry Meghan with having no news about Lucy so he'd decided to go to his house and retrieve his weapons bag. He'd kept one since leaving the SOA, but he had enough weapons in his bag to mount a defense to save her.

All he needed was a location and time to rescue her.

God, You brought Lucy into our lives for a reason. Please watch over her. Keep her safe until I can reach her.

He cringed when he thought about the terrible things he'd said to Lucy. Those couldn't be the last words he ever said to her. He wasn't sure he could live with that knowledge. He wanted a chance to apologize to her for lashing out and to make sure she knew how much he loved her. He wanted to marry her. He wanted to make her a permanent part of his and Meghan's lives.

He glanced at the phone on the seat, willing it to ring. He needed a location. Just a location, and he would bring this all to an end.

Finally, thankfully, the phone buzzed and he scooped it up. "Ross, do you have it?"

"We ran Paul's GPS and his car is parked at an old, abandoned factory on the south side of town. You know the one?"

He did, and he had the truck heading that way before Ross even finished talking.

"It's a perfect spot for what he's got planned. I'm gathering a team, but we're stretched thin here. I can meet you there in an hour."

"Lucy may not have an hour," Bryce told him. "I'm headed there now."

"I don't want to have to rescue you both."

"You won't have to do. I'll meet you there." He floored the accelerator and headed to the factory, praying he wouldn't be too late. Having a team with him would have been ideal, but he was prepared to go in alone, prepared to do whatever it took to save Lucy's life.

Father, make my aim straight and true and keep us both safe.

He cut his headlights when he reached the turnoff for the factory so he wouldn't draw attention to his arrival. The less Paul Summers knew, the better. He parked near Paul's car, grabbed his gun and hopped out.

He entered the building and heard voices coming from the back. He hurried through and ducked behind a large piece of equipment to scope out the area. Lucy was chained to the wall. Her face was bruised and her shirt stained with blood, but she was alive, and relief flooded him.

He wasn't too late.

And he wasn't leaving here without her.

He whispered a quick prayer before leaping to his feet and raising his gun at Paul. "Get away from her!" Bryce demanded. He didn't want to kill him if he didn't have to. He wanted this monster to stand trial for all the pain and grief he'd caused.

Paul spun to face him, knife in hand. He wasn't giving up easily. Instead, he reached for his own gun and fired. It zinged past Bryce and ricocheted off a piece of equipment. Bryce fired several shots, one hitting Paul in the leg. He grimaced and grabbed his leg, but that didn't stop him. He raised his gun again and started to fire, when Lucy suddenly kicked him, knocking Paul first to his knees, then kicking the gun from his hand.

Her sudden response had surprised Bryce as much as it had Paul, but the killer didn't wait. He reached for the gun again and turned it on Lucy, firing and hitting her in the stomach.

"No!" Bryce screamed and fired two shots, this time hitting Paul in the chest and head. The killer dropped the gun and fell backward.

Bryce ran over and kicked his gun out of reach, but when he checked on Paul he knew he wasn't getting back up.

Paul Summers was dead.

Bryce searched for the key to the chains and found it. He hurried over to Lucy.

"Hang on, Lucy. Help is on the way." He had her hands free in a heartbeat, then lowered her to the floor. She was losing blood fast from the wound Paul had inflicted. He checked her shoulder, but the stomach wound was more urgent. He took out his phone and dialed Ross. "I found Lucy. She's been shot. I need an ambulance."

"What about Summers?"

"He's dead." He dropped the phone and turned his attention back to Lucy. He did his best to stop the bleeding, all the while trying to keep her calm. "Hang on, Lucy. I'm here. You're going to be okay."

She reached up and touched his face. "Meghan?"

"She's fine. She's great. You saved her life."

She smiled and happy tears pooled in her eyes, but she had paled and was fading fast.

Where was that ambulance?

"I wanted to tell you something," she whispered to him.

"You don't need to say anything, Lucy. Save your strength. The ambulance is nearly here." He almost broke down with relief when he heard the sirens in the distance.

"Bryce." He turned his attention back to her. "I—I love you."

It was a simple declaration, but it meant everything to him. He touched her face and fought back his own overwhelming emotions. "I love you too, Lucy. Don't you dare leave me again."

He placed a kiss on her lips, but could do nothing else as she passed out in his arms.

Lucy needed surgery to remove the bullets Cassidy and Paul Summers had put in her, but it was successful, and two days later she was finally feeling better. Bryce and Meghan insisted on remaining with her while she was hospitalized, and she didn't protest. She was glad they were both there, and vowed she would never let them out of her sight again.

Lucy placed calls to her supervisor and her family to let them know she was okay. She was tired and in pain, but she'd made it out of her ordeal alive and was thankful that neither Paul Summers nor his daughter would be able to harm anyone again. Bryce had assured her he was gone, but he hadn't needed to. Lucy had seen him go down and known he wouldn't be getting back up. Yet she had so many unresolved questions, and was thankful when Detective Ross showed up for a visit.

"You look good," he said.

"I'm feeling much better."

He glanced at Bryce, then back at Lucy. "You'll both be glad to know that all charges against Clint have been dropped. He's been released and cleared in the murders of those women."

Bryce thanked him, but Lucy saw doubt behind his eyes. Yes, Clint had been cleared of the murders, but he still had Jessica's disappearance hanging over him. Until she was found, he would always be considered a killer.

"But not in the Jessica Nelson case," Lucy said, reading his expression.

Ross shrugged. "We still have no proof in that case one way or another."

Bryce addressed them both. "My brother told me he's been searching the lake. He's convinced she accidentally drove into it. He even found a necklace he says belonged to her."

"We sent divers in years ago, but that lake is so deep and murky that something could have been missed."

That gave Lucy an idea. "I have a friend at the FBI who specializes in water searches. I can ask him to check the lake again. I think they may find another victim of Cassidy's there too." She reached for Bryce's hand and gave it a squeeze as a silent show of support for Clint. Bryce's faith in his brother was now her faith too, and she would do whatever she could to help clear his name.

And speaking of clearing his name... "There's something I don't understand. If Cassidy was the one behind the attacks on me and Paul Summers was the Back Roads Killer, then why did the DNA results match Clint?"

Detective Ross gave her a knowing nod. "I wondered that too, so I did some digging and went back through the chain of custody of the sample given to the FBI."

She saw where he was going. "Someone tampered with the sample?"

"Yep. One of the lab techs is a second cousin to Jessica Nelson. He claims he was tired of seeing Clint get away with murder, so he swapped the real DNA sample with some he'd previously collected from Clint."

She shook her head. "If he was so sure Clint was guilty, then he wouldn't have needed to tamper with the DNA."

"That's true. There's no excuse for what he did, and Chief Dobson has been alerted. He's been placed on administrative leave pending a formal investigation."

"He also tainted any DNA evidence that might have been used against Paul Summers in court." She glanced at Bryce. "Although I suppose we don't need it any longer." There would be no court, no trial since Summers was dead.

Ross left and Bryce pulled his chair beside her bed. He held her hand and kissed it, and she lay back in the bed. She was finally safe. Everything had worked out.

"I love you, Lucy," he whispered. "I don't know what your plans are, but I hope you'll stick around for a while."

"I love you too," Lucy told him. She hadn't thought about her plans, but she knew she didn't want to leave Bryce or Meghan. She could envision her life here with them in Whitten. She didn't know yet how that would work out logistically with her job, but she knew they would figure it out.

She wasn't leaving his side again.

EPILOGUE

Lucy shuffled into the kitchen and poured herself a cup of coffee. The TV was on, and the news was still broadcasting the footage of Jessica Nelson's car being pulled from the bottom of Lake Klein, where it had been submerged for the past four years. Her body had been found in the driver's seat, still buckled in, and even Chief Dobson was claiming it looked like she'd driven off the road that night and drowned. He'd already appeared on television calling it a tragic accident.

Lucy was happy her colleague had finally been able to bring that case to a resolution and give the Nelsons much-needed closure. And Clint had been exonerated once and for all. He would no longer be forced to live under a shadow of suspicion.

She heard voices from outside and stepped out onto the porch. Meghan was riding Charlie in the corral and Bryce was watching from his perch on the split-rail fence. Their laughter was infectious and drew her toward them. This was her family now, and her home. Officially, she was working out of the Houston FBI office and clearing all the cases suspected of being the work of the Back Roads Killer. Most of it she could do from the comfort of her new home office so she could enjoy spending time with her new husband and stepdaughter.

As she approached the corral, Bryce hopped down and pulled her into his arms for a long kiss. "Morning," he said when the kiss ended. "You sure slept late. Long night?"

"Brutal." She and Jim Ross had spent hours interviewing Arlena Summers about when and where they had lived over the past twenty years. Finally free of her husband's controlling nature, she was cooperating fully with the investigation, but it had been well after midnight before Lucy made it home. "So far there have been confirmed victims in each city they lived."

A frown creased his face and she hated to tell him about the call that had awoken her this morning. "The FBI dive team found another car in the lake. A woman who vanished two years ago. Her family thought she'd run off, but…" She didn't even have to finish her sentence. She'd told him all about Cassidy's confessions of killing other women who'd dared to look at him.

He glanced in Meghan's direction, but Lucy suspected his mind wasn't on his daughter. He was still struggling to come to grips with his best friend being a cold-blooded killer. "I thought I knew evil. I thought I could look at someone and see their heart. I was wrong and it nearly cost me everyone I love."

She slid her hand into his and leaned against his strong shoulders. "Only God can see a person's heart. That's a lesson we both had to learn."

He nudged her with his shoulder and smiled. "We both got a second chance at that, didn't we?"

And that was what she hoped he would concentrate on instead of the terrible events of the past. "Yes, we most certainly did. A glorious, wonderful, grace-filled second chance."

He put his arms around her and pulled her to him, his kiss reminding her of all she'd gained since coming to this town.

The whinny of a horse interrupted their moment. Lucy looked up to see Charlie's head at the fence and Meghan sitting atop him sporting an annoyed look.

"I'm thirteen. No kid wants to see her mom and dad kissing all the time."

Lucy's breath caught at Meghan's new name for her—mom. But Bryce was having no part in her criticism. "Hey, weren't you the one who told me I was in love with Lucy and should marry her?"

Meghan shrugged as she led Charlie away from the fence. "Yeah, but I didn't know there was going to be so much kissing."

Lucy couldn't hold back the giggle that bubbled up inside her. "Should we stop for a while?"

But he shook his head. "I'll never stop kissing you, Lucy Tippitt."

And he sealed that promise with another kiss.

* * * * *

Watch for a new Love Inspired Suspense miniseries from Virginia Vaughan, coming soon!

Dear Reader,

Thanks so much for joining me in the final chapter of my Covert Operatives series. I'm sad to say goodbye to these characters, but I'm looking forward to a new series with new fun and exciting journeys.

I hope you enjoyed reading Bryce and Lucy's story as much as I enjoyed writing it. I loved the idea of taking an FBI profiler—someone trained to see and understand human behavior—and have her confidence thrown a curveball by something happening in her own life that she couldn't see. Her guilt over her fiancé's hidden addiction proved that her faith had been in her FBI training and her profiling skills. Ultimately, like we all do, she had to learn that only God can see and know all things.

I love hearing from my readers! You can contact me online through my website www.virginiavaughanonline.com or on Facebook at www.Facebook.com/ginvaughanbooks.

Blessings!
Virginia

Titus turned onto the paved road that led to town. Wren had said Ryan was there. Ambushed by the men who'd been trying to kill her.

He glanced in his rearview mirror and saw a car coming up fast behind him. No headlights. Just white paint gleaming in the moonlight.

"What's wrong?" Wren asked, shifting to look out the back window. "That's them," she murmured, her voice cold with anger or fear.

"Good. Let's see if we can lead them to the police."

"They'll run us off the road before then."

Probably, but the closer they were to help when it happened, the better off they'd be. He sped around a curve in the road, the white car closing the gap between them. It tapped his bumper, knocking the Jeep sideways.

He straightened, steering the Jeep back onto the road, and tried to accelerate into the next curve as he was rear-ended again.

This time, the force of the impact sent him spinning out of control. The Jeep glanced off a guardrail, bounced back onto the road and then off it, tumbling down into a creek and landing nose down in the soft creek bed.

He didn't have time to think about damage, to ask if Wren was okay or to make another call to 911. He knew the men in the car were going to come for them.

Come for *Wren*.

And he was going to make certain they didn't get her.

Don't miss
Falsely Accused *by Shirlee McCoy,*
available March 2020 wherever
Love Inspired Suspense books and ebooks are sold.

LoveInspired.com

Clang, clang, clang.

The hammering outside her new schoolhouse grew louder. Eva Coblentz moved to the window to locate the source of the clatter. Across the road she saw a man pounding on an ancient-looking piece of machinery with steel wheels and a scoop-like nose on the front end.

When he had the sheet of metal shaped to fit the front of the machine, he stood back to assess his work. He knelt and hammered on the shovel-like nose three more times. Satisfied, he gathered up his tools and started in her direction.

She stepped back from the window. Was he coming to the school? Why? Had he noticed her gawking? Perhaps he only wanted to welcome the new teacher, although his lack of a beard said he wasn't married.

She glanced around the room. Should she meet him by the door? That seemed too eager. Her eyes settled on the large desk at the front of the classroom. She should look as if she was ready for the school year to start. A professional attitude would put off any suggestion that she was interested in meeting single men.

Eva hurried to the desk, pulled out the chair and sat down as the outside door opened. The chair tipped over backward, sending her flailing. Her head hit the wall with a painful thud as she slid to the floor. Stunned, she slowly opened her eyes to see the man leaning over the desk.

He had the most beautiful gray eyes she'd ever beheld. They were rimmed with thick, dark lashes in stark contrast to the mop of curly, dark red hair springing out from beneath his straw hat. Tiny sparks of light whirled around him.

"I'm Willis Gingrich. Local blacksmith." He squatted beside her. "Can you tell me your name?"

The warmth and strength of his hand on her skin sent a sizzle of awareness along her nerve endings. "I'm Eva Coblentz. I am the new teacher and I'm fine now."

Don't miss
The Amish Teacher's Dilemma
by USA TODAY *bestselling author Patricia Davids,*
available March 2020 wherever
Love Inspired books and ebooks are sold.

LoveInspired.com

LIEXP0220